WHERE WHALES SPEAK

A TALE OF THE RECORD KEEPERS

by

Michael E. Morgan

WHERE WHALES SPEAK
A TALE OF THE RECORD KEEPERS

For information write to:
Dawn trader Books, LLC
PO Box 161
Wilton, Connecticut, 06897

If you are unable to order this book from your
local bookseller, or Amazon.com, you may order
directly from the publisher.
Quantity discounts for organizations are available.

Edited by Sal Glynn, San Francisco, Ca.

Cover and book design by
Michael E. Morgan
Publisher's Cataloging-in-Publication Data

ISBN
ISBN 978-1732-298-118
10 9 8 7 6 5 4 3 2 1

Table of Contents

The humpback whale is a species of the Baleen whale, one of the larger Narwhal species. Adults range in length from twelve to sixteen meters and weigh about twenty-five to thirty metric tons. The humpback has a distinctive body with pectoral fins that are very long. Its head is covered with knobby bumps and close to shore when migrating.

The whaling industry flourished in New England around the latter part of the eighteenth century to the middle of the nineteenth century. The commercialization of whale hunting began in the Atlantic Ocean. As the whale population decreased, hunting spread to the Pacific and the Arctic region.

Besides the value of whalebone for corsets and ambergris for perfume, the primary profits came from whale blubber cleaved from their bodies. After harvesting, the remaining carcasses were discarded to float away at sea. The slices of blubber were brought on board the sailing ships and returned to port. There, blubber smelting plants would convert the fat to oil for lamp illumination. The oil burned clean and without odor. Hunting the 'the water beast' was like any other animal hunted on land, with fur pelts sold for food and clothing. The 'water beast' was productive and useful to society, much like the hunting of buffalo by the natives for clothing, tee-pee making and meat for their tribes.

With the immigration of the white settlers, equipped with 'fire sticks' (long rifles), now would tip the balance of mutual supply and demand outmatching the natives with their bows and arrows. The news of the wholesale slaughter of the buffalo from moving trains as a sport, encouraged hunters to come from Europe to the plains to hunt buffalo for sport as well, until none were left.

So, it was with whaling. It seemed reasonable that these creatures of the open sea could rightly serve man to light his way through the night with the sacrifice of their lives.

The hunter mentality provided no indication that any of the animals on land or the mammals of the sea could or would resist such slaughter because their intelligence was merely a gift of instinct through evolution. Man being the dominant factor, sought to kill all creatures considered as part of the lower food chain for whatever purpose.

In the late 1930s, in excess of fifty thousand whales were killed annually. Then in 1946, the International Whaling Commission (IWC) was formed. They banned all commercial whaling. Despite this, Japan still whale hunts.

During this time, science emerged growing in all directions with the passion and zeal of the renaissance. Now the centers of academia began to wonder which species might be a closer-kin to the human. With the advent of Charles Darwin's book, *The Origin of Species*, suggested that man's origin might have sprung from our other primates, the apes, through something called evolution. This idea exploded into the modern world with a terrible controversy and a backlash of religious indignation.

In time, some scholar/explorers of experimental biology cautiously and quietly began to explore the scientific investigation of animal intelligence. Any attempts to publish their results would always end up in the garbage. Their more conservative colleagues sought to ruin their reputations and remove them from the mainstream flow of credible scientific pursuit.

During World War II, German U-boats attacked ships in supply routes on a regular basis. The Navy felt the need for a unique weapon that could travel faster under water than any ship including submarines. This weapon would move silently toward a target without detection and strike without warning. This idea was very different than a torpedo approach, which could be detected early by the whirr of its propellers.

The need suggested, in theory, an organic weapon delivered to an enemy craft by a water-born creature trained as an underwater soldier.

In 1960, the government research and development agency of the US Department of Defence became interested in the theoretical use of advanced marine life to support the war effort. A Naval research lab situated on the coast of California, sought to make use of the fast swimming bottle nose dolphins as suicide bombers. They tried to teach them how to attach themselves with limpet mines strapped to their backs to the bottom or sides of war ships.

Once again, no consideration was given to the possible resistance from friendly dolphins to join the conflict occurring between humans on the surface. There were several academic institutions involved, vying for the lucrative government contracts offered. Initial stipends were doled out to promising research labs.

One such Lab was part of The Massachusetts Institute of Technology-Woods Hole Oceanographic Institution Joint Program. Doctor David Janus, director of research at the facility, also functioned as professor, substituting some of his precious field research activities for mandatory classroom instruction at the university.

His latest published paper, 'The Theoretical Spatial Recognition Algorithms by Observed Interactions Between the Humpback Whale and the Bottlenose dolphin', qualified the university to receive a stipend from the government for his continued work.

Doctor Janus believed it was possible for human-cetacean or human-dolphin inter-species communications with these higher intelligent water-based mammals. The military applications of his work did not interest him as much as his passion to find an intimate link to these sea creatures.

The Department of the Navy tried to lure Doctor Janus to their marine laboratory in San Diego but he preferred to work from his closer domicile near the university. The Navy deferred to another expert in dolphin inter-species experimentation, one Doctor John Lilly instead.

From the whale perspective, there are two clans; the Elder Keeper clan of the Narwhals and the Messenger clan of the humpbacks. The Keeper clan is the keeper of all life records, all comings and goings of sentient life on this planet.

The Cetaceans were drawn to the main star of this binary system to teach the higher order of sentient life called Nom-Lu-Lu on an inhabited planet called Tiamat existing in the 5th orbit.

Many Hundreds of Thousands of Bindaars (in whale years, each Bindaar is equal to fifteen human years) passed before the man-child emerged. A rogue planet orbiting the twin sun Etere, a dwarf star of this solar system, collided with Tiamat in the fifth orbit leaving many small fragments and one large remnant. Much of the remains of Tiamat stayed in the fifth orbit of the main star now known as the asteroid belt.

The large remnant drifted out of the fifth orbit and into the third orbit.

After the collision, the Cetaceans decided to protect the few survivors and themselves by filling the remainder of Tiamat with water from their home world, a Blue Luminar. Their world, a water planet, orbited around their star Alaim Atare existing at the rim of the galaxy. Then they renamed the offling of Tiamat, Earth. Earth translated in the Cetacean language means 'little Tiamat.'

The Elder clan oversaw the entire remaining cetacean colony and have done so for Tens of Thousands of Bindaars. They have kept the records true and watched over all life developing on Earth. They felt the remaining survivors of Nom-Lu-Lu would best be served by merging their energy and tome with the early man-child.

They watched with horror as the man-child became bent and corrupted. Eventually the energy and consciousness of the Nom-Lu-Lu all became suppressed within their conscious presence.

The time has come to call for exposure, giving an opportunity to reach out to the man-child to seek and hold the rightness of harmonious living, to teach the man-child the memory of the 'way' or the Powah originating from the great mother world the cetaceans here called Plinahs Etere, also known by other outworlders as Tiamat.

The man-child must adhere to the 'way' if Plinahs Etere's idealogy is to endure on the Earth until the passing of Blue Luminar of Alaim Etare, at the galactic rim. When, in that time period, the Cetaceans will return to their home world, their purpose here will have been achieved.

A FRUITLESS EFFORT

Doctor Janus Diary Entry: July 2, 1965

The waves lap gently against me while I look desperately for any sign of success. At the end, another day is spent on the open sea without even a tale to tell of the 'big one' that got away.

I return home, waterlogged and exhausted. Before I even say hello to my wife, I am back at the charts on my desk, looking to map another search area for the next day's experiments. My wife Katie is only mildly supportive now, whereas in the beginning, she was more eager and enthusiastic about my work. Now she is often irritable and less patient with me to the point of being critical and perhaps doubtful about my sanity.

Day after day she grows weary of my fruitless efforts. I suspect she is perhaps mildly jealous of my other love, the dream of communicating with the whales. I know, she would rather have my undivided attention on her with the same passion I give to my dream. But I am helpless to offer her that promise. My only hope is that success will vindicate my ideas and raise my status with her and my colleagues to a much higher level.

Doctor Janus Diary Entry: July 4, 1965

I sit at my desk today, on holiday. My field work is at a standstill so, I make another entry…Hope springs eternal in man's darkest hour when all seems lost that the war effort looms larger. Our instincts lean toward something smarter, stronger and greater, something higher than ourselves. We dream of greater expression, made in our image, a perfection approaching the divine. I am not so deluded with that form of self-importance. Biology is my life, more specifically, marine biology, because it represents life in its greatest diversity. Life in the sea is always developing, experimenting and evolving higher forms out of the primordial slime that is its origin.

We struggle to prove, as primates, even to our own predecessors of a lesser nature, we are the superior of the species. Yet, I wonder, if that is so? Perhaps we humans enjoy this moment of success only because of a fortunate and perhaps serendipitous set of circumstances. I focus on, well obsess really, another form that does not change. It comes from another former line of evolution that may have actually reached perfection.

The faithful drop to their knees humbled and bewildered to learn that life answers the call with its greatest irony. Biology remains in my life and is my path to understand life in all of its wonder. It has always been my inner most belief that hope arises in the most unexpected places, not from above, but from below, in a form perhaps at the roots of our seed, not of land-walkers, but of the ancient ones, the great seafarers, the oldest and wisest living among us, the whales.

I am reminded of those other explorers who look up at the sky. Like me, they wistfully dream of fame and glory as they feverishly scan the skies with greater passion. They are convinced of their efforts to seek for signs of extraterrestrial life with their radio telescopes while stimulating a new hope for mankind and continue to remain for some, a viable pursuit.

Meanwhile, The Next Morning
MIT School of Marine Biology Lecture Room

The morning sunlight enhanced the details in

the carved structures placed around the grounds of the campus. Though these carved stone posts serve to define specific items of interest on campus, they are also inscribed with details and directions for those visiting. The students all know the campus well, where they are and need to be without the use of the standing posts. So, as useful as they may be by a few tourists, these stubby obelisks might as well be non-existent to anyone of the student population. The population on campus is transfixed on their individual aspirations and plans for their future. The beauty, grace and integrity often dismissed, falling into that unimportant category of consciousness called utility.

MIT Research Laboratories has among its faculty, some of the finest minds in the country. Building 24 housed the School of Marine Science and Biology. It is almost 10 a.m., and time for my morning lecture. The semi-round classroom, amphitheater style with rows of students banked high on three sides, all can peer down at the demonstration table. This class was designated for post graduate students seeking a Doctorate in their chosen field of work.

A large chalk board suspends from the back wall dimly lit from ambient light in the room. The room lights were off leaving the red exit signs to give an eerie illumination to the room. Below the demonstration table a row of hidden lights shown toward the floor, exaggerating the shadows above. On top of the table mounted a bottlenose dolphin replica. It was loosely covered by a thin shroud. The plastic animal parts could be removed in any sequence revealing hidden compartments, or other nonvisible organs important for study.

The buzz in the classroom subsided to a low hum of voices. All side conversations and inner thoughts would now cease. All eyes are forward with the anticipation for the appearance of the professor. His entrance was legendary among students and all were waiting for the performer to enter upon the stage. Then, with a certain magical bombastic entrance, Doctor Janus appeared simultaneously as the main lights are turned on. The blast of bright light from the depths of darkness, subjected everyone to temporary blindness. This gave Professor Janus an opportunity to shock everyone out of their smug egos long enough to get their attention.

Doctor David Janus removed the thin shroud quickly and dramatically the way magicians do during their reveal. A partially dissected dolphin replica sat on a mahogany base while he stood in front of the replica proudly. His hands gripped the display behind him. There were a few chuckles heard before he began.

"Today's lecture people, will be on the hollow cavity located just behind and below the nose and forebrain."

David's strength and athletic agility, minus his stature, defined his demeanor as a mature outdoor type. He was self-conscious with two small scars, one below the lower lip and the other beside his left eye. He hid a certain nervousness and insecurity which he experienced in front of crowds. He cloaked it with his bombastic behavior. It's all an act really. He believed in his act of hiding, but most students knew it. He always began with some reservations. When he got into the subject of whales, he transforms to speak confidently and passionately.

Unlike most professors, his class is always

filled up well before the semester begins. Some girls in the class fancy having a more intimate relationship with him, so they can beguile a better grade. He especially ignores their flirtations.

David continues as he points with a baton.

"The upper cavity is similar to the humpback… only smaller. It is used to generate the pops, clicks and siren sounds characteristic of their mutual exchange, especially during the mating rituals."

Several chuckles erupted and spread sporadically throughout the class, especially from the women.

David ignored the laughter and went on.

"Who can tell us another purpose of this cavity and appendage?"

Several hands rise into the air, mostly from the females. David scans the rows of students and picks Darlene, in the front.

Darlene began."Isn't that cavity used for the feeding call?"

David responds kindly.

"Well… yes in a manner of speaking. We have just begun to realize…the bottlenose dolphin will identify a school of fish, purportedly, dinner. Then alert the others in the area. Several dolphins will surround the school of fish and send out simultaneously… a burst of highly concentrated sound pulses that arrive at the center of the school of fish. The area of water explodes violently into cavitation. Then the dolphins move in and feed on the stunned fish."

There is a moment of silence as students squirm in their seats with mumbled discussion. Then David continued.

"We are just beginning…"

Then David is interrupted by another student, Gary, who is astonished by the information, now with his hand held high.

David responded.

"Yes Gary…"

"Sir… Gary began. I was wondering…how they would know…you know, I mean when to emit this sound together… I mean…without alerting the other fish?"

David responded.

"That is a very good question Gary. But remember…the dolphin is warm blooded, it is not a fish! The truth is…we're not sure exactly. We only know that to create such a disruption in the water their timing must be very precise.

And… David paused for dramatic effect. Then he smiled as he looked around for student's reactions. He continued. It is my belief that they communicate nonverbally!"

Then another student, Charles, chimed in.

"You mean to say…another sound high enough that cannot be heard by other fish?"

David responded.

"No Charles! I mean telepathic communication!"

Charles squirmed noticeably in his seat shifting between a slight smile and distress. Then more mumbled discussion occurred around him. Charles went on.

"You…cannot be serious… right… I mean fish…uh I mean mammals…they cannot do that… right?"

David continued.

"Yes Charles, I believe they can. Consider for example, the humpback whale… Its brain weighs more than forty pounds…that is five times the weight of the human brain. It also has hundreds more convolutions than the human brain, an attribute long held to determine maturity and greater levels of intelligence. You really think that all that brain power is just for finding and scooping up plankton?"

Now Gary jumps back into the discussion almost laughing.

"Wait…You mean to say that dolphins can talk…I mean carry on conversations, make plans, or even talk about their chicks?"

The class erupts into a roar of nervous laughter.

David responds and begins to laugh a little too.

"Well…David began with a smile, I am not sure if they exchange telephone numbers…"

The class breaks into laughter again.

He continued.

"It is my belief that all intelligent species communicate…and…it is possible that they may be able to do even more. Remember…they have been here a lot longer than man. Perhaps…just perhaps…in some cases…they may be even more intelligent than man!"

The silence in the room was deafening until the

class broke with the sound of the bell. Students descended the amphitheater chatting over David's statements.

Meanwhile deep within the Atlantic Ocean

Namoo and Lamoo, two mature humpbacks were idling by watching their two younger offspring swimming nearby.

Lahroo, the younger male asked.

"Remtah and I wondered about the man-child thrashing about on the surface, trying desperately to reach out to our kind."

Lamoo answered.

"Men children often thrash about on the surface in many places. It is something we have observed quite often from their kind."

Then Remtah chimed in.

"But father, Remtah petitioned, sometimes the sounds the man child makes are similar to our mating sounds! Do they want to mate with us?"

Lamoo moved alongside Remtah to comfort her.

"Oh, my no! she exclaimed. It is by chance that

the man child stumbles upon some of our mating calls. Actually, this particular man child is of some interest to the Fah Ne. The council has brought the attention of this man child to the Eternal Minoch for closer observation. No doubt he has generated a lot of attention from the council with his behavior. He does these actions many times, and on many days of his keeping. His persistence in doing this has many on the council quite curious.

I'm sure they have the matter well in view my child. We should allow the council to deliberate about this matter in their own wise time, blessed is the Feyh of the Eternal Minoch."

Lahroo would not let it go and persisted with more.

"But father why do they not allow us to communicate with this man child? Remtah and I have scanned him and found him with much kindness in his being and certainly worthy of our attention."

Before his father could respond, Lahroo continued with his argument.

"It seems sad to me that the Fah Ne would make such a rule not to interfere in men children's affaires. The Fah Ne decision seems stiff and cruel when the men children clearly need our wisdom and help!"

Lamoo's tone became strong and reprimanding.

"Your attitude regarding the Fah Ne is reprehensible. You need favorable guidance to regain your respect for the Fah Ne!"

Lahroo lowered his head to show recognition of his father's authority.

"I regret challenging their wisdom, but I am troubled by this way father and do not understand the gain of this way."

Lamoo moved along-side Lahroo to comfort him.

"You are young my son and it is understandable that you do not have the wisdom yet to embrace the vastness of the way yet. It will be many hundreds of bindaars until the wisdom can seek to fill your inner tome. Go to your nether place and meditate on the Eternal Minoch for your deeper comfort."

North Atlantic, the Barents Sea
Near the Aleutian Trench July 14,1965
1400-hours Zulu

Cascading sheets of rain blew against the rising swells of ocean with gale force winds. Beneath the violent surface the ocean seemed less effected as the depth increased. Eight-hundred meters below, stretches out into a vast and murky pale-green ocean. The panoramic view is accompanied by muddled sounds of the roaring silence mixed with the torrent swells clashing on the surface.

An additional sound became part of the mix for the humpback. A new sound, an unfamiliar sound, the whine of propellers beating furiously against the water, giving an early warning of a large thing quickly approaching. The entity emerged through its wash from strange swirling fins as a long gray bottle determined in its direction, never swerving, never deviating, never stopping. This thing was most strange, most curious. It had never before been seen or encountered at this depth.

The long gray shape happened to be a Triton

Class Atomic Submarine, the U.S.S. Scorpion. The submarine churned its way steadily through the Barents Sea toward the Aleutian Trench. As the craft moved through the water it ran silent except for the whine of its propellers and a faint ping heard along the port(left) side of the craft.

Inside the control room the panorama included; bow plane (dive) control, radio control, sonar control and the XO's(Executive Officer) station. The crew chatter rose only slightly above the background equipment noise in the room.

At the sonar station the pings were loud accompanied by a circular blue screen presenting a bright green line sweeping slowly around the display. Above, the blue screen, the digital display or oscilloscope, showed a wavy line on its smaller screen while the staccato chirping of highspeed printer heads pounded against the paper below, illustrating in computer code, the analysis of the ocean's landscape.

The chief sonar operator, seaman first class John J. Scully (aka JJ) listened to the signals on headphones while he studied a book on navigation for his next promotion. Scully was clean-cut and meticulous about his appearance, confident and quite accustomed to life aboard a submarine. He turned to pass along his interpretation of the sonar signals to the XO.

JJ called out.

"Exec Con..."

The executive officer, (aka Exec) Lieutenant Jiggs Sadler is the officer on deck, it is mid-watch and he is presently at the Con (control of operations). Jiggs likes to take risks and considers himself quite the poker player. He always chews on an unsmoked cigar. When he is nervous, he switches sides and bites on it.

Jiggs is in mid-discussion with chief Porter on the art of playing Blackjack.

Jiggs answered the alert from JJ on the com link.

"Exec…aye"

JJ continued.

"Sir…we are approaching the third course change."

Jiggs responded.

"Thank you…Mr. Scully."

Jiggs reached for the com link rotating the

switch to the skipper's ready room.

Jiggs pressed the call button.

"Skipper…Exec here."

Then the captain answered.

"Captain…aye."

Jiggs answered back.

"Skipper…we are coming up on the final course change."

The skipper responded.

"Thanks Jiggs…I'm on my way."

Meanwhile
MIT Marine Biology Lab Lecture Room

As professor Janus continued to elaborate on his ideas of intelligent species on the planet, two male students were chatting and laughing together, not paying much attention to the class. The first student, Walker, often expressed an indignant attitude toward Janus' ideas. Often, he joked about his class with friends outside of the class.

David felt irritated by Walker's obvious pompous behavior.

Then looked up at Walker with a slight smile

and a sarcastic tone.

"Mr. Walker…Perhaps you would care to share your humor with the rest of the class?"

Walker now caught off guard, responded with some arrogant surprise.

"Sir…?"

David grew more impatient as he watched Walker continuing to laugh at the apparent weakness presented from David's challenge.

Then David pushed back on Walker even further.

"Well, Mr. Walker…?"

Walker shifted from his casual position, leaning forward in his seat over the chair in front, while he stared down intently at David. He wanted to show David he was not backing down from the challenge. Walker's attitude was matched also by his size, he often used it to push others around. He relied heavily on his varsity position of the school's football team as protection from any of the Dean's reprimands.

Walker grimaced with a sardonic smile and responded.

"Well…What…Sir?"

Walker's challenge prompted David to look down breaking his glare with Walker. David looked around at the other students hoping that one of them might come to his defense, if need be. David looked up at Walker. Suddenly David's face relaxed as a euphony occurred to him.

David started in...

"What is the most important thing in your life right now Mr. Walker?"

Walker became confused looking for a way to defend against David's tact.

"Well…I guess playing football."

David did not like confrontation. He struggled to maintain his nonchalant aloofness. So, with that David continued.

"So…You like to play football."

Now, Walker doesn't respond. The smirk leaves Walker's face replaced by alarm.

David continued.

"And does not your scholarship require…that you pass my course with at least a C grade?"

Walker still remained silent. He slid back into his seat feeling threatened.

Walker spoke submissively.

"Yes sir…I don't want to…"

Then the classroom bell rang cutting off Walker's voice. The other students rushed toward the door creating a lot of clatter along with mumbled discussion. Walker turned to his friend John and said in a low voice.

"Oh…man…I thought that asshole was going to nail me…"

Walker peers over John's head to catch a glimpse of David eyeballing him on his way toward the door.

Then David called out over the noise to the students leaving.

"Don't forget to leave your assignments on the table…and that includes you Mr. Walker…"

Walker flipped his assignment onto the counter as he returned David's look in a measured defiance. Walker turned back to John and said.

"You know…he said in a low tone, I was sure he was going to kick my ass out…right here!

David continued over the noise.

"And…don't forget to read chapters 4 through 7 from Hornsby…I'll be in my office on Wednesday and not Tuesday."

John chortling to Walker.

"Man…You had better watch your ass…He had a hard-on for you today, and he continued on while chuckling…but you were saved by the bell!"

Meanwhile
Aboard the U.S.S. Scorpion

At the far end of the control room the forward hatch opened and the captain emerged. The Captain, Commander George Sanders (aka skipper) had served in two previous campaigns; one with the Japanese fleet in the pacific and one with the German destroyers in the Atlantic. He enjoyed nerves of steel as a seasoned submarine captain, commanding respect from his officers, as well as the men. His peppered-gray hair stood straight above his closely shaved sideburns. His eyebrows were bushy and partially covered his steel blue eyes, setting deep into his weathered leathery face. He appeared ruggedly handsome and sported a reputation amongst his friends in the officer's club as a lady-killer.

Jiggs yelled out, while coming to an attention

posture encouraging others to do the same.

"Officer on deck…and then turned to the skipper declaring, Sir you have the con."

The skipper returned sharply.

"As you were gentlemen…thank you Mr. Sadler."

The skipper is handed the duty roster and writes something in the watch log then hands the log to one of the ensigns saying.

"Son…I would like a hot cup of coffee… some cream…no sugar."

The ensign snapped to attention and responded.

"Aye Captain sir…right away sir."

The skipper moved to the chart table. A slight grin appeared on his face as he swept aside the blackjack deck. He looked at Jiggs with a slight disapproval. Jiggs turned beet red with embarrassment.

Jiggs silently mumbled.

"Oh shit…then he spoke out loud, Sorry sir."

The skipper then picked up the compass and began to study the charts carefully. While looking at the course data, he placed the compass across three points and rotated it twice along the charts for distance and bearing. Then he drew a line toward the trench.

The skipper then looked at Lieutenant Sadler and said.

"Left full rudder Mr. Sadler. Bring us around to bearing 217 Mark 2, Bow plane 2 degrees down bubble and all ahead one-half…steady as she goes."

Jiggs answered smartly.

"Aye sir…Helm, left full rudder, bearing 217 Mark 2…"

The helm then answered.

"Helm aye…217 Mark 2… sir."

Jiggs shouted to the bow plane control

"Bow plane…2 degrees down bubble"

"Bow plane control aye…2 degrees down bubble"

Then Jiggs issued the final command to the engine control room.

"Engine room…all ahead one-half…steady as she goes"

"Engine room aye…all ahead one-half…steady as she goes… sir."

Meanwhile

MIT Campus Outside of the Dean's office

Dean Haggler left his office harried. He approached the parking lot with purpose to his step. He starred at the ground as he walked trying not to draw any attention until reaching his car. He looked up to see David approaching and frowned. Then he looked at his watch impatiently knowing what was coming next.

David called out.

"Uh…Dean, glad to catch up to you before you left for the day. If I might have a word with you?"

Dean looked annoyed before he spoke.

"For the one-hundredth time…there has been no word…"

David lamented.

"But it has been months since I submitted my paper on the theory of cetacean pattern recognition and algorithms."

Dean consoled.

"David you have had a lot on your plate…I can understand that. Katie says it's been rough on you."

David reacted with surprise and some annoyance.

"You have been talking to my wife?"

Haggler said correcting David.

"You mean estranged wife, don't you?"

David eyed Haggler fiercely.

Haggler continued.

"Katie said she needed a break…and I thought you should give her some breathing room."

David answered sternly.

"Listen Haggler…I don't need your advice…I just need my grant!"

Haggler added while ignoring David's rant.

"David, she seemed desperate…San Diego was my idea…It was a good solution."

David again surprised.

"Oh…so San Diego was your idea… eh?"

Haggler stopped for a moment ignoring David's question.

"There was an opening for a cypher at the Naval base…So, I recommended that she take it."

Then Haggler impatiently glanced at his watch again. He placed his hand on David's shoulder attempting to console. Then he said softly.

"David, it's what she wanted."

David's eyes narrowed with anger as he swept Haggler's hand from his shoulder and said.

"How could you know what she wanted? From now on, butt out…and just get me my grant!"

Haggler said nothing. He shrugged his shoulders and walked away.

Meanwhile
In the U.S.S Scorpion Control Room

The low frequency flash receiver spewed out a message from the command center of the US Atlantic Submarine Pac Fleet. The radio control room operator Sparks, immediately hailed the skipper on the com link.

"Exec Con…"

"Captain aye…the skipper responded"

"Sparks here sir…Captain…I have just received a flash message from Atlantic Sub-Pac Fleet Headquarters…Sir."

"Send it up sparks"

"Aye…captain."

The skipper was sitting at the charts table when the ensign returned with the skipper's coffee and offered it to him. Then a seaman emerged into the control room and approached the chief with the flash message from Sparks. The chief briefly examined the flash message and handed it over to Jiggs.

Jiggs turned it over to the skipper.

"Skipper…your flash message."

"Thank you… Mr. Jiggs."

The skipper began to read the flash message as he slurped loudly on his coffee. The message read, *ALERT…OFFICIAL TOP SECRET EYES ONLY… July 15, 1965…1800 HOURS ZULU…FROM US ATLANTIC SUB PAC FLEET COMMAND HEADQUARTERS…MISSION CONFIRMATION CODE ALPHA…BRAVO…ALPHA…TANGO… BRAVO…TANGO…YOU ARE TO PROCEED TO THE ALEUTIANS…DEPLOY PROJECT BRIGHT EYE FOR TEST AND EVALUATION AND RETURN TO BASE…ADMIRAL H. JAINWAY COMMANDING.*

The skipper looked up at chief Porter and Jiggs.

"Do you confirm this message to be authentic Mr. Porter?"

"Aye…Skipper."

"Jiggs…Do you concur?"

"Aye…Skipper... The message is authentic."

"Very well…gentlemen. Secure Bright Eye for running."

A DREAM CRUSHED

Doctor Janus Diary Entry: July 15, 1965

They all think I'm crazy, but I will not give up. I have lost confidence from my colleagues and most of my funding has run out. Only a few of my graduate students are left that are willing to help. They sit in the boat quietly, listening to a hydrophone for hours upon hours, hearing nothing but my thrashing about in the saltwater. There is no payment for them other than a few cold beers in the cooler, and a promise of my professorial sanction to their doctorial theses.

My work is not altogether random however. I bang on a shallow metal tin and blow madly into a submergible whistle to a specific set of patterns based upon my theory of interactive algorithms almost every day. When there is no response, I relentlessly move on to the next set of patterns.

Later that Evening

It was late in the day. Darkness was approaching. Doctor Janus stopped his splashing, pounding and whistling. He turned to his devoted crew in the boat and said.

"Okay guys, that's it for today. We'll go ahead again tomorrow with the next set of patterns. I know you are tired of all this and it seems daunting, he said lamenting. Then he continued with an encouraging tone. But this kind of work is essential scientific endeavor. I will make mention of your considerable efforts in my recommendations toward your doctoral applications later on, despite the very real possibility, that my theories will not hold water...no pun intended here."

His students chuckled at his remark adding to grateful solace to an otherwise disappointing day for their professor.

"It's okay, Doctor Janus. William said. We'll keep trying as long as you need us to do so."

David smiled fondly toward William and to the rest of the crew and offered.

"Listen guys, why don't you take whatever beers are left in the cooler back to your frat house. Enjoy a few for me, you've earned it."

They all waved at David as they piled into the coupe roadster one after the other. The roadster belonged to Gerald, a wealthy hot rod enthusiast. David looked on silently admiring their youth as they sped away stirring up dust from the road. He opened the trunk of his pale-yellow Plymouth, dumping the wet gear into the remaining space. Beach sand sprinkled over a broken beach chair, along with some paint splattered clothing used on his cottage bungalow the summer before.

He started the engine sinking deep into thought. He wondered if Katie was right? Maybe he was chasing a doomed dream well underway to oblivion.

It's an hour's drive to his apartment, allowing plenty of time to sulk. This behavior gave time to consider all the insults and humiliation from colleagues. Finally, he weighed in on Katie's declaration. It was hard, to hear her words that cut deep into his heart. '*You are wasting your brilliant career on a childish dream, looking for validation and self-esteem along the way, and you are the jester and fool of the campus.*'

The hour's drive drifted into a stream of painful feelings reducing to a harsh reality of his loneliness. Now, only minutes away from the bungalow, David's thoughts jolted to a stop. He needed some essentials from a convenience store nearby.

His thoughts turned briefly from the abruptness of an unfulfilled dream and broken home. It seemed strangely kind. He could momentarily replace that empty place of sorrow with the need for supplies.

He methodically brought his Plymouth to a stop in one of many parking spots available in front. The glaring bright lights from inside the store were contrasted by a sign outside, flashing like a beacon. The first three letters missing from 'welcome' offered a cryptic message to any weary travelers seeking its refuge.

David dragged his body out of the car, the door swung partially open. His body revealed a deep ache as he walked. It was a familiar ache from fruitlessly pounding on the water. He tried desperately to call out to the one creature he believed would understand his agony. There in the water, his agony sang out as an unrequited lover's cry that no other human could feel.

Entering from the outer darkness into the

brightness of inside, suggested a change of dimension heralded by a small ringing sound. A dangling bell announced his presence to the proprietor sweeping the floor behind the counter.

It was Mrs. Itame who looked up, freely offering her cheerful smile. She greeted David with a warm welcome.

"Ah good evening Doctor Janus. Can we help you to find something?"

David broke out of his somber feelings and responded with a reluctant smile in return. He simply nodded.

"Just a few items this evening, thanks. He said. Then David picked up a small basket near the entrance and began to wonder the isles, randomly grabbing a loaf of bread, some strawberry jam and a half carton of eggs for breakfast. He added a small bottle of low fat milk, a can of planter's peanut trail mix and a frozen TV dinner. Passing by the fruit stand on the way to the checkout counter, he threw in a small Chinese pear and a green banana exclaiming,"okay. I think that will do it for me."

As Mrs. Itame began to ring up his purchases,

Mr. Itame emerged from the rear of the store carrying an assortment of carrots, bell peppers, and onions wrapped in a burlap bag. He expressed his delight to see David and warmly greeted him as well.

"Always good to see you Doctor Janus. How is Katie, we hardly ever see her these days. Is she well?"

Mr. Itame's innocent question seemed to echo in David's ears reverberating like a distant ocean buoy clanging with a mournful warning of shallow waters.

David held back his emotional trauma and responded flatly.

"Oh, she is fine. He said matter of factly. She has been away visiting some relatives for a time. I will tell her you inquired when she returns home."

Mrs. Itame frowned silently and sternly at her husband. Mr. Itame, getting on in years with memory fading, would often lack awareness of existing conditions around him.

As Mrs. Itame loaded the paper bag with David's purchases, she handed his change to him, adding.

"You have a good night and take care of yourself Doctor Janus. The night carries a chill these days and you won't want to catch a cold."

David smiled and said."Thanks. I'll be extra careful. You have a good night too."

David's bungalow sat perched above a slight incline from the street. There were several steps to climb before reaching the porch and front door. He fumbled with his keys, for a moment struggled to balance his bag of groceries while opening the door.

Once inside, he reached around for the small lamp sitting on the vestibule by the door. He dropped the keys and the bag down on the table and quickly halted the bag from falling over.

The lamp illuminated the main foyer just enough to indicate several boxes randomly stacked around the room. Some still open and partially unpacked. Some of the boxes contained some of Katie's things she hadn't taken with her. David promised to send them off to her place in San Diego. He kept hesitating to rush off the last remnants of her presence.

The room was sparsely populated with a

tattered cushioned chair next to a side-table facing a small television perched precariously on an unopened box.

He sat down in his chair after pulling the TV dinner from the bag. He left it on the table intending to put it into the toaster oven.

Suddenly, he felt a familiar pressure building up in his chest. With a sudden burst of coughing and wheezing, he began another episode of full-blown asthma. He suffered this affliction since childhood. It began shortly after the tragic death of his mother and father from an automobile accident at the age of six. Only his older sister was left to care for him. He kept a breathalyzer in his pocket always, with a spare on the fireplace mantle. After several inhalations, the attack finally subsided but left him exhausted.

His thoughts meandered for a while then burst onto the memory of that horrible night of their ferocious fight. She came home after a stressful day at work and felt testy. His memory ran like a movie epic before his mind.

He began to complain of his back pain which triggered another round of irritations regarding her frustrations of their struggling life together. His lack of financial security from the university, the lagging promise of the much needed funding boiled over with her annoyance of having to support their life together.

Katie opened the kitchen cabinet above her head. Two items fell ricocheting off her head and crashed to the floor. She declared. "Shit! Well that's just great."

David called out. "You okay?"

She retorted. "Just forget it okay."

Tears rolled freely down her cheeks softening her mascara. Standing pensive and silent her heels crunched through loose macaroni under her feet. Katie clutched onto a dish towel nearby and held it under cold water hoping to ease the throbbing pain on the side of her head.

An unusual amount of anger stirred as she continued to curse under her breath.

David arrived in the kitchen a little too late to comfort her. He extended his hands with arms outstretched to embrace her but she pushed him away.

"I'm fine, just fine. I don't need your help now!

As usual, I'm the one left to do everything around here!"

David capitulated. Are you hurt? Here, he gestured, let me..."

"No, it's nothing!" She snapped, brushing away his hand. Then she continued.

"With you it's always the same...nothing changes and I'm tired of it!"

David's head dropped. He looked at the floor dejected. He remained silent as Katie continued to rant. She was shocked as she erupted with even greater fury.

There...you see...you are doing it again. It's always about you, isn't it? Just once, I would like to come home and reveal how bad my day was, but no...I always have to hear your bullshit, your failures and conflicts first."

David wanted to respond, to say something but his reaction to her shouting shut him down. He couldn't help but to retreat like a deafmute seeking refuge within his self-pity.

David finally blurted out."Christ, I'm trying, if you'll just..." Then she interrupted.

"What give you more time...a little more

patience? I have no more time to give. You have used up all my patience David. Daddy was right! You're just a dreamer

And I'm wasting my time…and for what?"

David said in his defense."I know I'm close. Closer than ever. You know how important my work is to me!"

Katie stared at him silently. Her thoughts gelled quickly into something palpable she had not considered before. David was no longer the underdog she wanted to love and care for. He was simply a loser. A new determination suddenly moved over her. She headed for the closet and pulled out her suitcase swinging it onto the bed.

Desperate to halt her in her tracks, David lamented."Wait…Think about what you are doing Kate. We can work this out…we've always worked things out."

This time Katie was unmoved by David's pleading and continued to wildly pitch her clothing into the suitcase. Then she stopped momentarily.

David…Maybe it's time you woke up. Your work is going nowhere. My God David…you just don't see it. They are laughing at you…and me. What about me? You can waste your career David, but you are not going to waste mine. It's too late for us, but maybe not for me!"

Silence filled the bedroom with a deafening crunch as she slammed the suitcase closed and bolted from the bungalow slamming the front door.

Meanwhile in the Control Room Charts Table of the USS Scorpion

The Exec, Jiggs, informs the skipper of the Bright Eye system status.

"Skipper…Bright Eye is at the ready."

"Thank you Mr…" The skipper is suddenly cut off by the radio operator Sparks on the com link.

"Skipper…Sparks here sir."

"Skipper…aye"

"What is it Sparks?"

"Sir, I have a flash message from CINCLANFLT …Sir …It's Admiral Jainway on the horn Skipper."

"Okay Sparks…pipe him through…Hello Admiral, Captain Sanders here sir.

"Good to hear your voice Admiral."

"Captain are you in position?" Admiral Jainway enquired.

"Yes Admiral…We are ready to commence with project Bright Eye."

There is a brief pause with some crackling sounds over the com link and the skipper becomes annoyed as the radio continues to break up.

The skipper switches to Radio con. over the com link.

Radio con…

Radio con…aye

"Sparks! What hell is going on with the voice link on the com?"

"I don't know skipper. We are trying find the problem sir." Then the admiral's voice breaks in over the static.

"We are all with you son…more crackling static…and good luck to you…Jainway out" … then more static.

The skipper tries to respond."Thank you, Admiral. We'll do our best sir…Sparks get on that damn radio, its breaking up again,"

"Aye Skipper"

U.S.S. Scorpion control room

The skipper turned to Jiggs."Jiggs…"
"Aye Skipper…"
"Commence Operation Bright Eye…"
Jiggs responded."Aye Skipper"
Jiggs called out on the com link to the sonar room.
"Sonar room…"
"Sonar…Aye"
"Commence Bright Eye Operation…"
"Commencing Bright Eye…Aye"
The newly fitted port (left side) and starboard (right side) Bright Eye arrays began to rotate into position coupled with the sound of metal gears. Once in position, a humming sound indicated the power was applied. They began to vibrate a strong very high frequency phased electromagnetic field pulsing with a specific programmed pattern. The ocean began to ripple in response beyond the arrays in a complex pattern of small intersecting waves in response.

Open sea at the end of the Aleutian Trench

Two humpbacks, Lamoo and Namoo, tilted down nose to nose in the communing position near the zone of solitude at the end of the Cimarron corridor.

Many others are swimming near the entrance of the great undersea sea known as Shamranal. There is no attention paid to the strange object, the U.S.S Scorpion, approaching toward their domicile.

Sonar Bright Eye Station U.S.S Scorpion

The flat panel glows with a warm pink effervescence, buzzing and crackling with electrostatic charges. The air above the platform forms a dimly lit cloud with bright ribbons of color streaking through the cloud appearing as a miniature thunderstorm. Points of brighter light emerge slowly amidst the hue of pale green as the array jumps into focus. The crew standing by on the control deck stare in astonishment. Unlike the older system of sonar, with its green circular display, flat and only two dimensional, having a brighter green line slowly sweeping around the screen like a light house beacon sat in the corner switched off and silent.

The silence in the room suddenly broke into cheers and laughter. The new display revealed the entire ocean and all of its contents, all life forms and human vessels within range of the high frequency signal. The crew now realized what whales must be able to see.

Jiggs turned to the skipper.

"Congratulations skipper. I think we've Just made naval history sir."

The skipper turned to shake his hand, nodding with raised eyebrows while still staring at the display. The display was dazzling. It appeared like a mini aquarium of the open sea.

The skipper dropped his gaze and recovered quickly. Now the captain began with practical matters at hand, the complete testing of the Bright Eye system.

"Okay…Let's see how this baby works in tighter quarters.

"Jiggs…Two degrees right full rudder…"

"Aye captain…Helm…"

"Helm…aye"

Jiggs commanded."Two degrees right full

rudder…"

Then the skipper commanded Jiggs."All ahead one third."

Jiggs called out."Engine room…:

"Engine room…aye"

Jiggs repeated the command."All ahead one third…"

"Aye…All ahead one third."

The skipper then said to JJ."Give me a reading in the canyon…what does it look like so far?"

JJ responded. Sir…I'm getting some momentary spikes from the circuits on the port lateral array…but it's within nominal limits…sir."

The skipper paused…"Good…keep me informed…"

Then the captain arose from his chair at the con saying,"Jiggs, you have the con."

Jiggs responded."Aye… very well captain… Helm…Steady as she goes."

"helm… aye. Steady as she goes."

Open Sea at the End of the Cimarron Corridor

The Bright Eye signal spread out in all

directions causing thousands of disruptive ripples in a tide of seawater cavitation. The ripples reach the end of the canyon walls where the two humpbacks, Lamoo and Namoo began to lurch suddenly in great pain. Their huge hulks writhed and contorted as their minds struggled with the signal's explosive effects. Some humpbacks remained nearby, swimming around in circles in a frenzy, unable to approach or help.

The young ones, Lahroo and Remtah are frightened by their parent's weird movements and they were making agonizing sounds they have not heard them make before. They wanted to rush to their parent's aid, but they are warned away.

Lamoo strained to telepathically reach Lahroo…"Son stay clear there is something very bad here. Your mother and I are straining to defend against it. It is harmful to our kind, so do not approach us."

Then, Remtah noticed the strange long gray creature approaching quickly from the end of the canyon. She called to Lahroo."Brother, look! There at the end of the canyon, a monster is coming! I have never seen anything like that before. I feel that thing is looking to harm us and it is making our parents very sick. We need to use our new skill, maybe we can torqx and chase it away?"

Lahroo paused to get a better view of the long gray beast. He could see it was very large and very strange. Its movement was nothing like he had ever seen either. He tried to scan it but got nothing. He concluded the beast had the ability to resist their scanning. He thought, '*what kind of creature could resist their scanning?*'

There was little time to mount an attack, but he agreed it was definitely charging toward them.

Lahroo exclaimed."Yes, but our torqx ability is too weak to fend off the creature individually, so we will do it together."

Remtah agreed. They tilted down their noses until their tomes touched and began the special breathing and whistling sounds emitted in synchrony like their porpoise friends do to catch fish.

A great pressure began to build up before them until the salt water began to swirl around. The sea responded to their calling in a great whirling under water cyclone. As they continued to sing their torqx song to the sea, the sea water kept building in strength and became a tidal wave of spinning sea water moving quickly toward the Skipjack.

The U.S.S. Scorpion Bright Eye station

JJ noticed something odd. A blackness began to appear at one end of the display near the end of the canyon. It appeared to be growing and moving very fast. At first, he thought it was some sort of malfunction in the display. Then he realized it was moving very fast toward the Skipjack.

JJ grabbed the com link fast and called the Exec.

"Sonar con to the Exec."

"Exec…Aye...What is it JJ?"

"Sonar con here sir… There is something happening at the end of the trench sir. It's big…no bigger… and it's growing…It looks like some sort of special distortion sir…like you would see after a detonation sir!"

In that moment, Jiggs slams his hand over the general quarters alarm button and switches the com link to the skipper's ready room.

"Skipper…"

"Skipper…Aye…What's going on Jiggs?"

"Skipper you had better get up here sir… something is coming at us really fast!"

"I'm on my way…"

The holographic display at the Bright Eye control station grows darker every second, rapidly moving along the canyon walls moving ever closer to the submarine. Jigg's eyes widened with alarm as he looked at the display.

The skipper inquired nervously.

"JJ are you sure this is not a system malfunction?"

JJ responded nervously.

"Yes sir…all systems are nominal."

Jiggs climbs the ladder smartly leading to the control deck. The forward hatch opens quickly leading from the captain's ready room and the skipper emerges.

Jiggs turns to call out.

"Officer on deck…Sir you have the con."

The Skipper responded.

"Thank you, Mr. Sadler…As you were…Okay

what's up Jiggs?"

Jiggs began to explain with tension in his voice.

"Well, we don't know sir…telemetry isn't confirmed…based on the display parameter, it's big and moving fast sir."

Jiggs removes his hat to wipe the sweat from his brow, followed by a shift of his unlit cigar to the other side of his mouth. The Skipper switches the com link to the Sonar Con.

Sonar Con…

"Sonar Con…Aye"

"I need analysis now Mr. Scully!"

"Sonar…Aye…The computer is working the numbers now sir."

At the Sonar Bright Eye station the printer heads pound away as the paper pushes out in a stepped like fashion synchronous with the lines of numbers printed, with the paper folding over the catch bin revealing the new computer data.

"Well Mr. Scully?" The Skipper pleaded forcefully.

"Aye captain…The computer data says the anomaly range is 12,000 yards and closing…at a rate of 750 Knots sir."

The Skipper frowned!

"Mr. Scully…Did I hear that right? Did you say the anomaly speed was 750 knots?" The skipper mumbles under his breath… "750 knots! What the hell! It's no torpedo explosion, nothing can move that fast for that long!"

The sea churns violently from all sides of the canyon, twisting and turning like a tornado. A dense tidal wall of sea water continues to follow just behind the churning toward the submarine. The sea water makes an eerie groaning and rumbling sound as if the water itself was angry.

JJ goes back to the com link calling the execcon.

"Sonar con…"

The Skipper responds.

"Exec…Aye"

"Sonar…Aye…Sir the computer analysis makes it a wall of sea water! … It's mean density is 1200 atmospheres … and the speed is increasing to 900 knots sir!"

The skipper's expression turns pale as his mouth falls open.

"Sonar Con…"

"Sonar Con…Aye"

"Mr. Scully…if that computer is correct about 1200 atmospheres… that will crush us like a tin can! Then the skipper called for fire control on the com.

"Fire Control…"

"Fire Control…Aye"

The Skipper yells loudly."Load aft tubes 1,3,5,6 and set the telemetry detonation for 10 seconds." He turns to Jiggs."This party is over boys, let's get the hell out of here… Right full rudder Mr. Jiggs… and come about smartly to bearing mark 115 mark 4…Blow all ballast…and 10 degrees up bubble."

Jiggs began to repeat the Skipper's commands.

"Helm…"

"Helm…Aye"

"Right full rudder…Bearing 115 mark 4…come about smartly."

"Helm…Right full rudder…Bearing 115 mark 4…coming about smartly…Aye"

"Bow Plane…"

"Bow Plane…Aye"

"10 degrees up bubble and blow all ballast.

"Bow Plane…10 degrees up bubble and

blowing all ballast…Aye"

"Fire Control…"

"Fire Control…Aye"

"Open aft tubes…1, 3, 5, 6 and check telemetry for detonation in 10 seconds."

"Fire control…aft tubes 1,3,5,6, loaded and open …set for 10 seconds detonation…Aye."

The Scorpion tilts upward toward the surface rapidly followed by a loud creaking sound coming from its hull. The crew braces for the steep angle.

The skipper calls out to Jiggs. "All ahead flanking speed Mr. Sadler."

Jiggs moves his cigar to opposite side of his mouth and bites down.

"Aye…Skipper"

"Engine room…"

"Engine room…Aye"

"All ahead flanking speed."

"Engine room…All ahead flanking speed… Aye."

Then the Skipper said finally.

"Fire control…"

"Fire control…Aye."

"Fire control, ready on my mark…5…4…3…

2…1…Mark!"

"Fire control…4 fish away sir."

The Scorpion is smothered in a rush of bubbles as the forward and aft ballast tanks are released. The submarine tries to out run the massive watery assault. The wall of dense sea water is splayed by the 4 explosions, but it moves forward undaunted. The crew stands holding on to anything nearby waiting to know of their fate.

The Skipper called sonar con on the com link.

"Sonar con…"

"Sonar con…Aye"

"Well JJ… did we at least slow it down?"

"Sonar con…I'm afraid not sir…range is now 2500 yards and still closing at 900 knots sir."

The skipper turns the com link to radio con.

"Radio Con…"

"Radio Con…Aye…sparks here sir."

"Sparks…Do we have that radio working yet son?"

Sparks lowers his head before answering.

"Sorry sir…It' just giving me fits …sir."

The Skipper lowers his head shaking it negatively for a moment and then looks at Jiggs mournfully tightening his lips and expressing futility. Jiggs rolls his eyes back for a moment, realizing their fate and shifts his cigar once more to the other side of his mouth biting hard.

The skipper somberly tells Jiggs."We can't use the ELF to flash a message of our position…better make ready the marker buoy…and launch it."

Jiggs paused for a moment before responding.

"Aye Skipper…Chief of the watch…make ready the buoy…launch on my mark. 3…2…1…mark"

Chief of the watch then said, "Buoy is away sir."

The North Atlantic, Barents Sea

The Scorpion is overtaken at 18:30 hours Zulu, July 15, 1965. The hull implodes from the aft bulkheads moving forward rapidly at one station at a time. The submarine rolls over onto its side in a downward descent to the sea floor spewing forth oil and debris. All hands are lost.

The marker buoy emerges on the surface moments later, blinking with a bright blue-white light accompanied by a staccato bleep occurring every few seconds.

Washington DC, The White House

Many important government people gathered in the Vice President's ready room. The issue of the mysterious loss of a Triton class submarine in the North Atlantic is on the table for discussion.

Tensions escalated more since the discovery of U2 flights over Russia. In addition, several field agents' identities of the CIA and NSA have been revealed in Germany. With their lives in danger, they extracted and recalled them as a result of a security leak from MI5 in London.

The U2 plane flown by Francis Gary powers was shot down by the Russians in 1960. The capture of Powers, being publicly charged with espionage, along with an embarrassing public trial in Russia made matters worse in the so-called 'cold war' with Russia.

Those present at the meeting were, Vice President Simon Potter; Secretary of State Jordan Hicks; head of Naval Intelligence Commander Jack Straker; Senator Howard Diensbach, Senator George Halder along with the Chairman of the Joint Ways and Means committee, Garin Hardy;

the Secretary of Defense Admiral Charles Holland and the Naval Joint Chief Rear Admiral James Cameron represented Naval military concerns.

The Naval joint chief Admiral Cameron expressed concern the Russians may have been involved and wanted to move the military alert status from Defcon 4 to Defcon 3. This idea became very controversial with several members of the group. Tempers at the meeting began to flare.

Vice president Potter sat on a short tan Victorian couch facing the other members of the meeting, looking beyond a mahogany coffee table littered with half empty coffee cups. Sitting next to the Vice President was the white house stenographer, Gloria Stephanopolis, busy recording the elements of the members' discussion together…the text restricted to 'for your eyes only' top secret.

The Vice President began the meeting.

"Good morning gentlemen…I wish this meeting were happening under less dire circumstances as we face this morning. I'll get to the point…At approximately 18:30 hours on July

15, just 43 hours ago, one of our subs, the U.S.S. Scorpion, went down in the North Atlantic with all hands lost.

"It is my understanding that this ship carried state of the art surveillance equipment and a full complement of Trident missiles!"

The vice president Looked up from his notes scowling over half framed glasses draped low on the end of his nose.

The Vice President continued."I believe that I am not alone to embrace the seriousness and concern this situation poses…Yes?"

The Rear Admiral Cameron interrupted the Vice President.

"Mr. Vice President…I am informed that a search and rescue sub designed for nuclear accident retrieval, is already at the site and removed half of the missiles on board. I expect to confirm all missiles are accounted for and properly stowed in a secure area on a designated Air Force base within the next 48 hours…Sir."

The Vice President responded."Well, thank you for that intel Admiral Cameron. At least we can say that we are half safe!"

The Admiral did not enjoy the Vice President's remark. He frowned while negatively shaking his head and lips tightened below his bristling mustache.

It is well known around the Capitol, and up on the 'hill'(congress), the Vice president enjoyed using his biting sarcasm whenever and wherever he could.

Then the Vice president shifted his focus on the surveillance equipment on board the submarine.

"I believe that Naval intelligence has something to tell us regarding the safeguarding of proprietary surveillance equipment also aboard the U.S.S. Scorpion Submarine."

Head of Naval Intelligence, Commander Jack Straker stood up pulling files from his briefcase.

"Yes…Mr. Vice President…gentlemen.

According to our intel with the recovered data from the Scorpion, we are facing a new enemy… and it has a new and formidable weapon."

Straker pointed to the Major handling the slide projector.

"Major if you will…"

The projector screen illuminated with photos of

the downed submarine indicating specifics regarding the aft hull.

Straker continued.

"These are the aft views of the Scorpion taken 12 hours ago…As you can see…the aft rupture to the hull is folded inward. This suggests an external force, not an internal explosion. So, we can rule out a nuclear accident or an internal hull breach! This external force was strong enough to crush the hull. The Scorpion's hull was designed to withstand the normal forces expected from known depth charges launched by an enemy in combat at close quarters, meaning within 10 meters of the hull."

Mumbled discussion began between several members of the group.

Senator Halder inquired.

"Has an unknown faction within one of the other powers slipped in something new?"

Commander Straker responded quickly.

"As far as we know, no other known power has any technology available to cause this kind of damage. The surveillance technology aboard the Scorpion was designed specifically to overcome certain sonar problems encountered in areas like the Cimarron canyon.

"The secret mission was to test this new equipment in an area known for standard sonar reflectivity issues. This new system was designed to recreate and simulate cetacean abilities to navigate in such deep-water areas with seabed obstructions such as the high canyon walls near the Barents Straits."

Then senator Diensbach interrupted.

"You mentioned cetacean simulation. Isn't that some sort of whale species Commander?"

Commander Straker moved to answer the senator kindly.

"Yes senator, you are correct. Our new algorithms are based upon years of research of cetacean behavior and the equipment called Bright Eye reproduces these specific patterns used by humpback whales during their migrations."

Then Senator Hardy began to wrap his pen on his briefing notes.

"Commander Straker…I seem to remember a thesis on my desk many months ago suggesting the very same cetacean algorithms! Why do you present this proprietary information as something new when it is already in the public domain?

I believe, if memory serves Commander, it was a concept developed by Dr. David Janus from MIT, who was looking for funding at the time for further development!"

Straker was caught off guard but recovered quickly.

"Actually Senator, we were already working on this project long before Dr. Janus suggested a similar idea in his thesis. We had certain technical issues which we were able to overcome with the addition of some details outlined in Janus' thesis."

Senator Hardy became irritated by Commander Straker's skirting the issue.

"Well in my opinion, we should have the real scientist who developed this idea to testify before this meeting with his learned expertise on this subject, would you not agree Commander?"

Straker felt trapped by senator Hardy's suggestion and reluctantly capitulated to his request.

Vice President Potter turned to the others and declared.

"Gentlemen, let us suspend this meeting for the time being and arrange to have Doctor Janus immediately subpoenaed to Washington to testify, so we will reconvene at that time. Do you all agree with this decision?"

Everyone nodded in the affirmative.

Vice President Potter then declared.

"All right gentlemen…I move to adjourn this meeting until Wednesday morning at 9 a.m."

Meanwhile
MIT School of Marine Biology Lab Classroom

David is lecturing on the migration patterns of the humpback whale as Dean Haggler appears at the classroom door. Haggler walks over to David and whispers into his ear. David looks puzzled as Haggler walks out of the classroom.

MIT Marine Biology Lab Janus' Office

The door to David's office unlocks and David enters the room with his briefcase tucked under his arm awkwardly. Two government agents already sit waiting inside. David turns and is jolted by their presence.

"I guess Haggler let you in huh? He said smiling nervously. So, what's this about eh? Don't remember running any stop signs lately! He added sarcastically.

The agents stand and look at each other, surprised.

"Doctor Janus we presume…politely tipping their wide brim black hats… we are not the local police. Doctor Janus, didn't Dean Haggler tell you?"

David frowns as he begins to take files out of his briefcase and stuff them into a filing cabinet.

"Tell me what…exactly?"

Both agents look at each other again, puzzled.

The first agent spoke.

"Why…we are here to escort you to Washington for a briefing."

David continued to be coy.

"Briefing? …About what?"

Now the second agent spoke.

"Well, we don't have clearance to answer that question sir."

David answered with some alarm.

"You mean right now?"

The first agent responded.

"Yes sir…right now!"

David spoke pleading.

"I can't leave…I have classes."

Now both agents looked at David with a firm and serious expression.

Speaking in a grim tone the first agent added.

We have our orders Doctor Janus…This is not a request!"

The second agent mentioned. "Our car is waiting. Don't forget your notes and thesis Doctor."

The government car pulled up after negotiating some traffic near the pentagon. The two agents get out and assisted Doctor Janus to exit the rear door of the vehicle.

The Pentagon Washington DC
The Pentagon Joint Chiefs Briefing Room

After climbing a Mount Everest of steps to the pentagon building entrance, David passed by several security guards possessing automatic weapons upon entering the building, double glass doors clicked loudly to open.

There was a security station poised to receive him after entering. He had to shed his coat as well as, his briefcase for scanning. Beyond the security station, the entry desk lay just beyond. The desk is filled with a broad semi-circle console of monitor screens occupied by a Major, demanding that he sign in.

David looked around to see more security guards posted at strategic points around the lobby. He picked up the pen and scribbled his name on the screen. It shifted to an orange display indicating the acceptance of his signature. The agents continued on each side with their escorting protocol. Once he was in front of the doors leading to the conference room, the agents fell away like booster rockets leaving him standing alone to enter the conference room.

He paused to weigh the seriousness of his situation. A small tremor of nervousness rattled through his body in recognition of the immensity of the circumstances.

Again, more military police flank both sides of the entrance as he entered the large oval room which is dimly lit with a large map of the world hanging on the back wall, overshadowing the mahogany oval table sprawled before him.

Small lamps shrouded by emerald green covers sat in front of each station around the table, marked by leather-bound chairs, already filled with government officials of every rank and file of the government. As he entered meekly, all eyes turned to greet him officially.

All of the Joint Chiefs present sit to the left of the Vice President, Simon Potter and the Secretary of State, Jordan Hicks on his right. David is seated opposite Commander Jack Straker, head of Naval Intelligence. After he sits down, he noticed a thick folder laying on the table in front of him. The thick brief labeled 'Operation Bright Eye', with top secret stamped, in red across the title.

As David scanned the members present, he did not recognize many of those present. Senators, Howard Diensbach and George Halder as well as, Chairman Garin Hardy of the Joint Ways and Means Committee sit to the right of the Chief of

Staff, Admiral Jainway who also sits to the right of the Vice president.

The Admiral is spit and polished all the way, wearing his uniform smartly as if he were still a cadet. His dignity and experience are displayed handsomely by the spread of medals posted on his uniform. He often speaks softly but means business.

The Vice President spoke first.

"Admiral Jainway…and other distinguished members of this august meeting, we have the good Doctor David Janus here with us today to help us understand the nature and gravity of our situation."

David raises his hand shyly to acknowledge all those present. The Admiral nods toward David before the gavel falls hitting the base with a loud snap.

The Vice President spoke.

"Let this hearing come to order. I will test the patience of those who have already been witness to the facts of this situation…repeating what has already been stated…"

"Gentlemen…at approximately 18:30 hours on July 15, 1965, one of our subs, the U.S.S Scorpion went down in the North Atlantic. It carried state of the art surveillance equipment and a full complement of trident missiles with all hands lost. As of today fortunately, due to urgent rescue operations, the missiles have been retrieved and are presently secured at a non-disclosed air base in the US. The conditions for this tragic circumstance have yet to be determined. We are here to determine how this could have happened."

David looked around the room, wondering why he is there.

The Admiral turns to Commander Jack Straker.

"Commander Straker you may proceed."

Straker stands and began pulling files from his briefcase.

"Gentlemen…As I have said before, we are facing a formidable enemy. Using a heretofore unknown technology, has brought down one of our latest and finest boats."

Air Force Joint Chief, General Thomas Greer stated.

"Perhaps we are facing another terrorist attack?"

Commander Straker responded.

"No, with respect general Greer, the CIA has confirmed…the evidence points elsewhere… Now…

Straker picks up the blue document…presenting it to the group.

"If you will please open your briefs to page 12…I'll give you some background."

"Three years ago, a team led by Doctor Raymond Foliar at Lockheed-Martin proposed a new concept for an advanced submarine sonar surveillance system…DARPA allocated the funds…the project was code named Bright Eye. Twelve months ago, the prototype was built except…they could not make it work because of a flaw in the software. Then…we received Doctor Janus' submission on cetacean pattern recognition…and with that, we were able to develop…"

Then Admiral Jainway interrupted.

"You'll forgive us for our ignorance Commander, but what exactly is a cetacean?"

At this point David's mouth falls open as he realizes the fate of his paper. He butts in quietly before Commander Straker could answer.

"It's a whale …sir."

Straker continues.

"You see gentlemen…the Scorpion's mission was to run trials for Bright Eye near the canyons of the Aleutians, an area known for sonar reflection anomalies."

Admiral Jainway inquired.

"Do we know…exactly…what happened to the Scorpion Commander?"

Straker responded.

"Yes sir…I believe we have a pretty good idea…it seems that it was a coordinated assault using sea water as a weapon."

Vice president chimed in.

"Did you say… sea water Commander?"

Straker responded.

"Yes sir, Mr. Vice president…sea water…in the form of a wormhole!"

Secretary of State Hicks then said.

"Wormhole…Are you kidding…what do you take us for Commander? …I think you leave a great deal to the imagination…in fact…it sounds like pure fiction to me…what we are talking about here…little green men or sea monsters?"

Everyone begins to chuckle.

Straker trying to recover.

"Yes…I mean no…not sea monsters… whales…it's the whales sir, they are the enemy?"

The room falls silent for a moment, followed by silent mumbling.

Senator Hardy speaks out.

"You must be joking!"

General Greer piped in.

"You can't be serious?... Really… you're talking about fish Commander!"

Now David stands to correct the general.

"No general…not fish, they're warm blooded, they're mammals, like us…not fish!"

Then David pauses for a moment, as an insight comes together.

Of course, …It all makes perfect sense, he thought to himself'

Admiral Jainway responds.

"You care to add something Doctor Janus?"

David wipes his sweaty hands on his slightly wrinkled sports jacket.

"I'm beginning to understand…Now I know why I'm here…It's exactly what I've been saying all along, but nobody would listen…"

Now David hesitates, realizing that his day in court has finally come. David looks at the Admiral and the rest of the group.

"Well…My theory suggests some of the larger mammals, such as the bottlenose dolphin and the humpback whale are sufficiently intelligent to carry out sophisticated activities…manipulation of sea water is exactly what they do."

Vice President Potter exclaims.

"Would somebody please tell me what the hell is a wormhole?"

David begins to explain.

"A wormhole Mr. Vice President is a theoretically conceived bridge between two boundaries of space…a kind of time-space warp or short circuit between those boundaries…it's called an Einstein-Rosen bridge, stemming from the mathematical work of Dr. Nathan Rosen and Albert Einstein in 1935…Does anybody have a white board?"

The Admiral motions for the Major to get a white board from the adjacent hall. Soon the Major returns with the board and sets it up in front of the group beside David. David begins to draw a graphic illustration of the wormhole and continues.

"It's only been a theoretical concept until now…David mumbles to himself *'this is fantastic'*…then outwardly to the Admiral and the others, this could be…the greatest discovery and opportunity of a lifetime…So here are the two boundaries…they could conceivably connect and exchange energy…here, as he points to the diagram shown on the board. Perhaps the submarine got in the way of some humpback whales attempting to connect…"

Admiral Jainway interrupted.

"Doctor…with all due respect, are you saying that whales created and coordinated such a force in the ocean just to make a telephone call?"

David smiled sheepishly.

"Well sir…it seems abundantly clear, you've stumbled onto this force with your submarine!"

The group began to argue with each other heatedly.

Air Force Joint Chief General Greer then spoke.

"Well…I think the other people in this room would agree, the fact stands…we lost a valuable piece of hardware. I for one, think this is crazy! If we launch an assault on a bunch of whales, we'll be the laughing stock."

More mumbling arose within the group with some heads nodding in agreement and the Vice President also joined the Air Force General's suggestion of blowback from congress as well as, the general public.

Then Vice President Potter chimed in.

"Before I make my recommendations to the President Admiral, I'm going to need more proof!"

David tries to offset the element of fear in the room.

"In my experience and research of mammals, there is no evidence to date that whales or any other mammals have ever been aggressive…if anything…I believe it's an act of self-defense."

General Greer retaliates.

"Self-defense! …I suppose you know what these creatures are thinking? (The general catches himself) Uh…that is, if they can think."

David responds.

"Well…no general, but I feel I do know about their behavior…and I cannot accept they would do something like this unless they were somehow provoked."

The Admiral interrupts the clash between General Greer and Doctor Janus.

"Gentlemen…I think we have enough material for the moment…perhaps it's prudent to wait for more evidence before we recommend military action. This meeting should adjourn, don't you agree Mr. Vice President?"

Vice President Potter nodded to confirm Admiral Jainway's suggestion.

David nods in agreement toward the Admiral and takes his seat. Then the Admiral added.

"Uh…Doctor Janus, I'd like you to stay for a bit longer if you don't mind?"

The room empties leaving only David and the Admiral. The Admiral motions for David to take a seat closer to him and began confidentially.

"Son you certainly ruffled a few feathers today…"

David leans forward in his chair looking at the Admiral squarely.

"Admiral…may I be frank with you sir?"

Admiral Jainway nodded."Of course, son."

"Admiral…I know I'm right about this…but I cannot prove it yet."

Admiral Jainway smiled.

"Well, there are a lot of people around here with fingers quick to point…but I'm inclined to believe you…that said, I can't ask them to accept this at face value, regardless of your experience and credentials. We need to find out what these creatures are up to…we need someone with the skill to develop a backroom dialogue with these mammals…and I believe you are the only one who can do it if it can be done, Doctor Janus."

David added quickly with excitement.

"I'm going to need a facility to do this…and some top people in the field…some very expensive equipment…it's going to cost you a lot Admiral… perhaps millions."

Admiral Jainway leaned back in his chair massaging his chin and looking pensive.

"I do have some pull with the Chairman of the Ways and Means Committee,

Hardy and I go way back…then he leaned forward grinning…Yes, yes, of course son, whatever it takes…will you take a check?"

City-Central, Near the Grand Banks
of Newfoundland

The Elders of the great cetacean council, known as Fah Ne, gathered to discuss the altercation between the man-child and their deep-water machine.

Gandaloo Fah, the great Chief Elder of the Narwhal, gathered all the members of the grand council to their city central, Lamishaa Ne. Those present included Ramaloo, Sithaloo and Falwardoo of the Saglek Plain; Miamartoo, Analaroo, and Bandermaloo of the Demerara Plain; Shiinaroo, Petraloo and Lammaoo of the Ceara Plain and Quaradoo, Keenalaroo and Darasaloo of the Pernambuco Plain.

It was decided that before the situation becomes worse, an attempt will be made to determine the intensions of the man-child with their new infernal machine that threatens the extinction of the entire cetacean population.

Gandaloo began.

"When the man-child began to hunt our kind with their long spears and wooden surface ships 15

Bindaars before this time period, we agreed to sympathize with their brutal behavior and gladly sacrificed a few of our kind for their sake, hoping they would come to change their tomes after witnessing the devastation and brutality of their actions.

"We removed most of the population to Shamranal, the secret undersea sea. This action gave them the impression they had exhausted the supply of cetaceans available for slaughter.

"Then we were encouraged and hopeful when the man-child made laws to prohibit hunting our kind 3 Bindaars before this time period. We are greatly concerned to see the man-child reversing their tomes once again. Now something has changed with their behavior and it seems filled with much darkness.

"This time they are beyond the use of their crude long spears and wooden surface ships driven by the wind. They learned to move below the surface in strange ships made of metal driven by whirling blades that allow them to move quickly and stay below for an indefinite time. They are also using more efficient methods to harm our kind. Worst of all, it seems they are not interested to make use of their catch. Instead, they want to hunt just for sport!"

Gandaloo now changed his thought.

"Where are the offlings of Lamoo and Namoo? May their tomes rest within the great Minoch and may it always be the will of the Feyh, that change will come and that change will continue."

Sidoo Tu, one of the messenger clan from Pernambuco moved forward to offer information regarding the offlings.

"Great Gandaloo Fah, Chief Elder keeper of the Feyh, I am informed that three Manatu (bottle nose dolphins) are now escorting the offlings, Remtah and Lahroo to the city-center for fair witness before the grand council. They will be here very soon."

Gandaloo Fah uttered a deep tome response sounding a bit like a forlorn whine, followed by several short pops and clicks.

The three manatu appeared at the archway of Shamranal, the city-center, with Remtah and Lahroo in tow. They only learned of the great city-center by their parents Lamoo and Namoo when they were much younger. It was a story entangled with wonderful tales of its history and magical wonder, leaving them with an almost fairytale impression. They never, in their wildest imagination, expected to see and meet with the grand council no less the Great Chief Elder of the Norwhal Keeper Clan in paseel (together in person).

Gandaloo sent a powerful thought to the young ones to come forward. Lahroo felt the pull in his tome and his brain vibrated strongly. He turned to his sister Remtah and said to her."They need us to move closer."

Remtah was not yet developed enough to hear the telepathic vibrations clearly and relied on her brother for that until she was older and better prepared.

Gandaloo Fah spoke openly, realizing the younger female could not easily read Gandaloo's telepathic machinations.

"Do you grasp the seriousness of your action young ones? As he spoke, he could feel their anguish in the loss of their parents.

"We are deeply saddened about your mother

and father, they are known to us and their devotion to the Fah ne. They are in high esteem and revered among your clan. You both are honored by their keeping of you.

"Yet your actions with the man-child and his great under sea machine beast has caused great consternation among us, though you are offlings, your actions have endangered us all.

"Perhaps it is to your parent's credit that you could call forth the power of the Torqx at such a young age. I feel strongly, that they also included in your training only those in your clan that are well prepared to Torqx with wisdom and only for long distance communications with others of the far plains many thousands of denahs (a measure of distance by the length of a whale's body-head to tail) away."

At this point, Lahroo tried to use his telepathic ability, but Gandaloo interrupted him exclaiming.

"Speak plainly my son, so that all can hear the weight of your tome. Your telepathic skill is but a small range, too weak to be heard by all present."

Lahroo started to speak but Remtah interrupted him exclaiming.

"Great Father Keeper, we only wanted to chase the black beast monster away. When my brother tried to scan the beast, it did not respond. I for one, was frightened and believed it to be a mindless monster coming to attack our clan. We meant no harm. We did not know it was a man-child beast. We could feel the great anguish of our parent's agony. It was my idea to Torqx."

Gandaloo peered into Remtah's tome and felt the truth of her speaking, yet he quickly reminded them both.

"You are both responsible young ones because neither of you have the potency to accomplish conjuring the force of the Torqx by yourselves, and so you joined your tomes to conjure the force together."

Then Lahroo tried to defend his sister.

"Great Father Keeper, I alone should be punished because I took the lead even though my sister joined me in doing so."

"It is of no importance or consequence that you initiated the lead. As a male, that is your nature and the female will follow, this is the way of our kind, it is the way of the Feyh. It is the way that is always, the unfolding of that which is the one seed, the seed that grows and joins the soul of the Plinahs Etere and the Sohern Fah Ne. It is eternal and fixed within the great rim, that place of our origins and that place of our transition to the re-emergence into the Eternal Minoch (the Quantum Void.)"

Gandaloo Fah paused for a moment in deep meditation within the Eternal Minoch. Then he spoke again.

"The wisdom of the Eternal Minoch has spoken. It is clear that blame and restitution for your actions is not the order of the Feyh. Instead, we will provide greater loving guidance and proper training suitable for your level of skill, So, you will remain here in the city-central under the care of the manatu and those chosen from the Narwhal clan to bring about your education and further development."

The manatu rushed in and escorted Lahroo and Remtah away to the place of their keeping.

Gandaloo Fah spoke again.

"Members of the council and all my brothers and sisters of all the clans, our decisions from now on are at the least precarious and even dangerous, we must move with caution. I fear there is retaliation appearing on the horizon and we cannot afford a conflict with the man-child at this time period, it is not in the way of the Feyh. Yet it is urgent that we find a way to communicate with the man-child before matters get out hand.

"The Eternal Minoch has informed me there is a man-child that may be able to make a joining with our tomes. The messenger clan is aware of him and he shows great kindness and understanding beyond his clan. To be safe and cautious, I am asking all clans go to Shamranal for now.

"I will ask only one from the messenger clan to remain behind, to be the one to to make contact with this man-child. The task will be lonely, dangerous and difficult.

"First, this messenger must find this man-child, but I am told that he often comes to places where the land joins the sea. This is hopeful. The next problem is the precise nature of the way the messenger can communicate with the man-child. In many ways, he is ignorant of our language and does not possess telepathic ability and that is troublesome however, the messenger clan is often quite clever in these machinations."

"I will ask Sidoo Tu to be our liaison and has the most important task to learn of the Man-child's intentions."

All of the cetaceans then left the city-center Lamishaa Ne and headed for their secret undersea sea, Shamranal.

Gandaloo Fah called telepathically for Sidoo-Tu to come near. When Sidoo Tu arrived, Gandaloo explained the mission that he wanted Sidoo Tu to accomplish. He warned Sidoo about the hardships that Sidoo might encounter along the way and that he would be hunted and offered advice as to the way he might avoid any confrontation with the dark man-child until he reached the good man-child.

The Gandaloo Fah then immediately entered into deep meditation with the Eternal Minoch while Sidoo Tu stood by waiting. When he awakened from his meditation, he revealed what the Eternal Minoch had to say regarding making contact. Gandaloo said.

"Sidoo… the Eternal Minoch revealed to me the man-child has developed a curious form of communications the man-child uses to make announcements to his kind. It may suggest a way for you to contact the good man-child when you find him. It is something the man-child calls radio.

"There is one problem however. It seems there are two kinds of radio. One kind actually makes the Eternal Minoch vibrate, but the second form does not. You will need to make sure you are telepathic with the first form and not the second. The second form uses something else that does not vibrate the Eternal Minoch, so it will not carry your telepathic energy to the good man-child."

Sidoo Tu squealed with several clicks to show his excitement. Then he acknowledged his understanding of the instructions with a telepathic response.

Sidoo Tu began to swirl and dive showing his respect to the great Norwhal Elder Keeper and telepathically thanked him for the opportunity to serve the Elder Clan with such honor and as he turned to head for the open sea, he chanted the Eternal Minoch hymn asking for its blessing as he moved off into the vast green abyss.

Sidoo Tu began telepathically.

"May it always be the will of the Feyh that change will come and changes will continue. May our essence prolong the Feyh till the passing. May the soul-orb of Plinahs Etere ascend to the Sohrn Feyh Ne. May the Solar logoi Supreme connect us to the Napas Fah. In the joining there is only one. In the joining the one becomes all. May the all will to continue."

Sidoo Tu was mindful of Gandaloo Fah's thoughts and his warnings. He aligned himself to become vigilant of the possible dangers in his journey and quest to find the good man-child. As he made his way toward the barrier between the landfall and the ocean, his thoughts turned to this curious way of communicating amongst the man-child.

He wondered how he might be able to discern the strange differences between the two forms of radio. He felt some doubt in the ability to find the right form when he eventually discovers the home place of the good man-child. His ability to find the right form may make the difference between success and failure in his mission and in the end, the fate of all cetaceans.

Central Intelligence Agency, Langley, Virginia
Office of Sidney Bidel, Director

The Director, Sidney Bidel, sat in his office, in front of his computer examining the progress of certain field agents tasked with reconnaissance in western Europe.

Unlike the last director, he is quietly reserved but is quite bombastic when he gets angry. He dresses very smartly, paying attention to the latest in power suit fashions. He keeps his jewelry hidden out of plane view. While at home, he gives a very different perspective. Though some of his peers feel he is a liability, he does get things handled and taken care of efficiently. So, in the moment, no one wants to rock the boat about looking for a new director. The impression of his co-workers, he is all business and formalities. There is no sign of frivolity and definitely lacks a sense of humor.

Sidney leans in on his hunches. Following up on his latest hunch, looking for evidence of terrorist activity relating to white supremacy groups and or their many sub-group associates in

America.

He was reviewing certain clandestine operations within the past three years to identify certain Taliban factions linked with known criminal suspects identified by inner agency contacts from Interpol.

Agent Clark wrapped on his office door lightly.

"Excuse me sir, may I have a word with you? Something came up that I thought you need to know."

Bidel looked up at Clark and nodded for him to enter.

"What is it Clark?" He said abruptly.

"Well sir, Since the recent events regarding the Triton submarine disaster, we received several memos and email traffic from the department of defense. As you know, all memos and emails that are classified are tracked by the cyber security division. The Navy department has issued a priority one message that all ships scan the known migration patterns of whales sir."

Bidel responded.

"What is so unusual about that. That was to be expected Clark! It's part of the Naval project

'Impact".

Clark returned.

"Yes sir, of course. But first, the whale population seems to be disappearing off the radar sir. Another more pressing issue is, we got a red flag that someone attempted to hack into the Naval security division, trying to downloaded contents of one of their secured email servers."

Bidel tightened his lips.

"Do we know what the level of the breach is?"

Clark frowned.

"We are communicating with the Naval department now sir, they are on alert and promised to let us know what kind of data was obtained."

Bidel said firmly.

"Stay on it Clark, MI5 screwed us before by allowing their system to be compromised and forced several of our agents to be recalled from the field. We gave the Brits hell for that! Now we are going to look like idiots if we suffer the same. You get my drift?"

"Got it sir. I will keep you informed."

Two hours Later

Clark appeared at Bidel's door again.

"As you requested sir…I have an update from the Navy department. As far as they are concerned, only one item of data was obtained. It was from the office of Commander Straker. A trace was placed on the Commander's radio phone. The phone used was unsecured sir.

The call was made from a bar just around the corner from his office, apparently to an adjutant assistant. It was mostly small talk, but he was talking about hunting the whales… sir. The commander apparently complained the idea was preposterous, in his opinion…sir…maybe he was just spreading misinformation?"

Bidel visibly relieved said.

"Possibly…Okay Clark. Doesn't sound like anything serious to worry about. I'm sure the Navy will give him a proper slap on the wrist!"

Clark responded. Yes sir, I'm sure you are right."

Next Day

Clark got on the phone with Bidel.

"Sir we are monitoring global communications traffic on military activity from key allies. There seems to be multiple plans underway for naval exercises from France, England and Germany in the Atlantic… sir."

Bidel inquired.

"Are these exercises jointly organized?"

Clark revealed.

"Apparently not sir. Each country launched their own planned exercises independently."

"Have there been any formal announcements about these exercises?" Bedel pressed.

Clark continued.

"Well sir…when asked through official channels, they are doing this now because they felt it was time to do it!"

Bidel scratched his head and brushed back what was left of his thinning hair for a moment.

"Strange…I wonder if they are also onto our hunt for the whales? Has there been any leak with regard to the Navy's discovery about the whales' abilities?"

Clark responded.

"Well…Not…not that we are aware of…sir."

Bidel countered.

"All right Clark. I'm going to talk with the Joint Chiefs this afternoon and see what they have to say."

Later, The Office of the Joint Chiefs
Admiral Jainway Commanding

The hall outside of Jainway's office spread out into two but opposite directions. Due to the nature of the design, one could not get an accurate sense of the distance along each path of the hall.

Despite his rank and status within the military and his chumming with Washington's elite, he was quite satisfied with less. He expressed what might be perceived as an austere environment, beginning with the antique curved walnut bench parked against the wall outside his office.

This is where you would wait for a brief encounter with the admiral's secretary. She would always say, 'you'll have to wait until the Admiral is ready and calls for you.' Then she would tell you, pointing to the walnut bench, 'Meanwhile, you may have a seat here.' This would happen each time, no matter how often you visited.

Then, after waiting for a small eternity, the Admiral's secretary returned and declared, as previously stated, 'the Admiral is ready to see you now.'

It was an unspoken rigid protocol that Sidney Bidel was quite familiar with. He often met with the Admiral many times during any given week.

The secretary opened the Admiral's inner door for Sidney. The Admiral was sitting at his desk, working on lighting his favorite pipe. For a moment, he expressed a frown at the fact his matches kept going out too soon. The third try became a success and his facial expression softened. He turned in his swivel chair to face Sidney.

"Well Sidney, what can I do for one of my best political analytics."

His pipe now stoked, several large puffs of blue smoke rose into the air, filling the room. Sidney gazed at the Admiral. For a brief moment, he compared him to an old-fashioned steam locomotive puffing its way up a steep hill.

That image faded quickly as he remembered the

urgency of his question.

Bidel thought. *'What the hell is everybody doing in the middle of the Atlantic?*

"Good afternoon Admiral. Bidel began. There are many reports saying several Naval forces from the Nato Pact countries are independently going through military exercises at the same time, in the middle of the Atlantic? Is anybody worried in your department about what that looks like to our adversaries?"

The Admiral was far less troubled by the news that Sidney was offering. In fact, he seemed quite nonchalant about it.

He smiled as he removed a private stash of malt scotch from his desk side drawer. Then pressed his secretary's call button.

"Susan…be a good girl… bring us two shot glasses."

Her voice returned on the intercom meekly.

"Right away Admiral."

As he poured a slim level of scotch into the glasses, he picked one up and handed to Sidney."Have a seat Sidney" He said, as he grasped the other glass firmly smiling just before taking a sip.

Unprompted, the Admiral said snidely.

"So, you really think they are performing military exercises? It's an obvious cover up to hide their bid for the next prize, the whale technology!

"Oh, don't get your shorts in an uproar Sidney! It is inevitable really. After I convinced senator Hardy to fund Dr. Janus' new project, code named 'Impact', I knew we could not keep this discovery under our hat for long. It would only be a matter of time before the intelligence community around the world would realize what we are up to. So now, it's a free for all. To the winner gets the prize, a whale to poke and prod for all its secrets."

"Actually, the Japanese may have a running start on all of us. They ignored the unilateral commission on the ban of whaling 30 years ago. Actually, designed to prevent the whales from suffering the same fate as the mighty buffalo.

"It's ironic don't you think. With all of man's technical ingenuity accomplished in this century, he can still be outfoxed by one of God's simple creatures. If those creatures can bring down one of our most sophisticated pieces of hardware then, I believe they can outsmart us all!

"Sidney…I feel I am a good judge of character and a descent poker player. My money is on Janus! With any luck, he might just able to pull this off. Let's hope for all our sakes, he can learn to negotiate with those animals."

After a pause, the Admiral continued.

"Let us hope Janus finds the answer… before anyone else does. Otherwise, Naval supremacy on the high seas will forever be changed.

Meanwhile, in the Sea of Japan
Archipelago of Sakhalin

The Japanese whaling trawler, the Nisshin Maru, is now in route for the waters of the Tasman sea, off the coast of New Zealand. The Maru tracked reports of humpbacks sighted recently and described by the Australian department of Aquatic Ecological Consultancy.

Sidoo Tu, still in search for the good man-child, joined a pod of whales on their way to the undersea retreat. He inquired if they had noted any man-child thrashing about mimicking whale calls near any of the coastal waters they frequented recently.

The whales were curious about this request, but glad to report no such experience in their travels. Sidoo Tu thanked them for their communing with him and was about to depart for another area of the sea when the engines of the Nisshin Maru approached.

As Sidoo turned to bid the pod fair well, one of the whales suddenly screeched in pain when a harpoon struck its tail. Blood gushed into the water from the wound as the humpback wriggled to get free unsuccessfully.

Sidoo Tu narrowly escaped a second harpoon that plunged violently into the water near him. Sidoo mesmerized and alarmed to see these strange objects repeatedly entering the water, threatening him and the rest of the pod. He realized with his life now in mortal danger, to descend quickly to a deeper level.

He paused to watch the devastation occurring above him. He wept for the deaths of his new-found friends and offered a prayer to the Eternal Minoch to receive their tortured tomes.

Sidoo continued on with his determined search for the good man-child. He felt the mission now took on a grim reality, he remembered within his tome the warning from Gandaloo Fah.

He wondered what other dangers he might encounter along the way. Fearing these waters were precarious, he decided to change direction from his plan to enter the south china sea and leave the pacific waters behind. Instead, he began to swim north and further west toward the Monterey Canyon near the western shores of California. This area was known to the whale population as a pleasant and often fruitful place to find plankton, his favorite meal. All this traveling made him hungry and he was eager to eat.

The seabed rose steadily toward the coast from the canyon. He noted many strange white tubular objects oddly drifting by and resting on top and within some of the coral beds. He wondered if they were some new variety of food, but these clear luminescent objects did not swim lively, rather they seemed hollow and lifeless. This did not seem appealing. Sidoo decided to ignore these odd lifeless things and moved on, but the ache within his stomach grew stronger and reminded him that he needed to eat soon.

Most of the whales now rested within the undersea sea leaving the oceans devoid of his kind. It felt very lonely for him. Sidoo hoped that his search would end soon. He longed to see his family and friends again. Then he wondered if he would ever find this good man-child. The search seemed endless and often hopeless. Undaunted by this enormous task, he pushed on struggling to keep his faith in the Feyh that would guide him.

Naval Research laboratory
San Diego, California

Katie was hard at work concentrating on cyphers. This was her specialty.

She was thrilled to be working in her preferred field. While on the east coast, her primary task was supervision of those who were skilled in the art of cyphers, but still in training from her. She grew weary of teaching and desperately wanted to get back into the work herself. She welcomed the opportunity when Dean Haggler mentioned the opening at the lab in San Diego. Commander Straker was in charge of the lab and was grateful that she agreed to come.

She respected Straker and admittedly attracted to his forceful take charge behavior, a refreshing change from her husband David.

One day Commander Straker entered her office and greeted her warmly.

"So, how is it working with us now Mrs. Janus?"

Katie responded with some humility and corrected him softly.

"You can call me Katie, if that is okay with you? All my friends at work called me that."

Straker smiled and said.

"Well that's fine with me. Besides, we try to keep an informal atmosphere in the lab. I find it to be a better more profitable atmosphere to do this kind of research. You okay with your not seeing David these days?"

Katie anticipating Straker's fishing for her loyalties responded.

"Oh yeah. I'm okay with it. No problem really." She confirmed.

Silently, she winced thinking to herself. *'In truth, I do miss him.'*

Straker started to leave and turned.

"By the way, a few of us are getting together at the officer's club tonight. I could pick you up…say around 7?"

Katie touched by his offer, responded sheepishly.

"Sure! I'd love to."

Straker smiled broadly and added.

"Okay…Great, 7 it is."

Katie's thoughts tossed the idea around of

fraternizing with the boss. She pondered if she was embarking on tricky ground. Besides there loomed a slight sense of guilt having some fun without the consideration of David. She wondered how he might feel if he knew about it. He always expressed a certain jealousy when other men made casual compliments in her direction.

Later that evening, at the Naval Officer's Club

On either side of the Naval officer's club glass door, two MPs stood at parade rest guarding the entrance. Katie and Commander Straker exited the first military sedan and behind was a second sedan filled with two of her colleagues and two officer friends from Straker's office.

As Katie ascended the steps she stopped to view the ocean.

Straker turned to say.

"You okay, anything wrong?"

She gripped her gown raising the bottom edge so she could clear the last step.

"No. I could not ignore the smell of the Pacific salt air here. It's quite different than the smell of the Atlantic back east. I wonder why that is!"

Then both guards saluted the Commander smartly. The one on the left opened the glass door bidding them welcome.

The building outside, draped on the left with old sea faring equipment like sail blocks and tackle from the ancient four mast clipper days, draped with a course brown well-worn net. The rough whitewashed color of the building bore in front, several pier pilons with heavy rope dangling between each, providing the appearance of a sailor's port.

Once inside, a plush carpet embroidered with a large marine insignia colored with subdued golden hues contrasted the blue color spreading out on the floor in front of the huge bar.

The carpet led into a wide elegant quasi-circular room with a panoramic view of the ocean, dotted with many small tables covered in white linen tablecloths. A piano played softly in the background perched on a low performance pedestal on the other side of the bar. Later in the evening, the piano would swing back allowing a live band to play jazz music for the crowd.

The waiters were dressed in Navy whites customary to receive officers on deck, with small aprons draped from their hips. After Straker and Katie were seated at their table and the other members of the party seated as well, they were greeted by their waiter who began to say.

"Would you like your usual beverage Commander?

Commander Straker responded.

"Tonight…is a special occasion. We'll have a bottle of your best bubbly, if you will."

The waiter tilted his body in a slight dip forward acknowledging the Commander's request.

"Very good sir…" He said. Then promptly left.

Katie turned to Straker.

"My…she commented. The appearance of the club is quite deceiving from the outside. Once inside, it has all the appearance of a first-class restaurant in New York, minus the obvious military accents of course."

"The boys who renovated this place are retired marines and really into the nostalgia of old sailing ships. The cuisine in the kitchen is well beyond a galley kitchen, probably the best on the west coast, especially the sea food. I'm sure you will find pleasing to your pallet, my dear." Straker replied softly.

After finishing the blackened sea bass entree. Commander Straker looked at Katie and suggested with a grin.

"So, how about a round of drinks for everyone."

Katie leaned back dabbing her mouth at the corners.

"Oh my…I think the champagne was more than enough for me. I am basically a cheap drunk." she admitted, as her face blushed slightly.

Straker added a slight frown.

"You must have one more with me. Come on… he pleaded, have pity on an old sailor who doesn't like to drink alone."

Katie bit on her lower lip briefly, something she would do when she was caught in a situation that made her uncomfortable.

"Oh okay, if you must. But just one." She insisted.

Straker motioned for the waiter.

"We'll have two martinis, very dry please."

The waiter smiled with a nod."Right away sir"

"From my vantage point…Straker went on…I think you will be a great asset to us all. I can tell… He assured her…Everyone really likes and respects you. They tell me your work is pure genius. I think you are going to fit right in, you belong here Katie."

"She became flustered."Oh…you say that to all the girls I bet!"

For a moment, she became pensive. Her expression softened as she thought of David. Commander Straker took notice of her change of mood.

"What's on your mind love."

"Well…when I drink I become a little melancholic. I was just wondering how David is getting along." She replied.

Straker thinking he could take her mind away from her husband added.

"The latest scuttlebutt around the base is Dr. Janus is doing very well actually. The word is, he received substantial funding from the Navy. He is building a new lab somewhere in Maryland I think."

Katie looked shocked. The news left her speechless for a moment. She was confused and a little high from the martini.

"Wow…that's great…I'm glad to hear things have finally turned around for him. When I left to come to San Diego, I left him in a desperate state. I was actually concerned for his welfare."

Straker continued.

"Well…now you no longer have to worry about your husband. He'll be fine."

The club announced last call for drinks. Straker turned to Katie and made an encouraging glance suggesting one more for the road. She declined exclaiming.

"I'm sorry…it's late for me" and added.

"I'm an early riser. Besides, I'm very close to solving another part of the cypher I've been working on."

Straker expressed sarcastic lament.

"Ah well…no play time for my best scientist… and dedicated to her work!

Then he added.

"Okay, maybe next time." He said grinning.

Katie returned to her quarters peeling off her

evening shawl and tossed it on the couch. After closing the door behind her with her left foot, she kicked off her heels leaving them strewn underneath the living room coffee table. Still feeling dizzy, stared lovingly at her bed through the bedroom door.

This behavior was not like her. She was always neat to a fault.

She thought. *'Katie...my love, you are trashed!'*
She entered the bedroom and sat on the edge of the bed. She mentally resolved to take her clothes off and exchange them for her comfy pajamas, but fell back on the bed telling herself. *'I'll just take a little nap.'* Soon the nap turned into deep sleep curled neatly around her pillow.

Morning of the Next Day

Katie arrived early at the lab. She opened the front door to see she was first to arrive. So, began the process of turning on the lights and activating all the computers from sleep mode. Then began the frantic search for coffee. Opening cabinets all around the coffee machine, needing some welcomed caffeine to wash away the morning fog penetrating her brain. Without a first cup of Joe, kept her less than efficient. She needed it like yesterday, making up for the luxury of the previous night.

She sat at her bench and logged onto her computer. On a hunch, she opened the drawer on the left and rummaged around through note pads and pencils. There was a small tea box with one tea bag left. Her eyes widened. Tea was not her first choice, but tea did contain caffeine.

'Beggars cannot be choosers' she thought.

She waited impatiently for the tap water to heat up. Just as she poured the cup with medium hot water and stirred the bag watching the clear water turn color, she heard the from door open.

It was Sam, one of her colleagues who yelled.

"Anybody want coffee?"

'Figures!' She mumbled under her breath. Then poured out the cup into the sink.

Katie's focus was not up to her usual par. She tried to blame it on the previous night's outing. She realized hearing the news about David stirred old feelings. The urge to call him continued to grow while her work slowed to a crawl. She decided to break the ice and call him on her lunch break.

A small luncheonette existed down the road from the lab. It seemed an appropriate clandestine place to make her call. Upon entering the dinette, she spied for a booth at the end of the counter, where she could enjoy a little privacy.

She pulled her phone from her bag noticing her hand shook a little. A clear sign her confidence was not what she expected. A moment went by trying prepare for how she would approach this awkward moment. Then, she began dialing David's number. The operator interrupted her call exclaiming.

"The number you have dialed is no longer in service."

At first, she was disappointed. Then realized, Straker said.

'I think he is building a lab in Maryland.'

She called the operator and requested that the she search for Dr. David Janus in the Maryland directory. The operator reported that she could not find the listing she wanted. Now Katie was frustrated. Then she paused to calm her feelings and tried to focus on a solution.

Then she asked the operator to give her the Naval Base directory in Maryland.

The base operator answered.

"NSA Bethesda Naval Air Station Operator speaking, how may I direct your call?"

Katie began.

"Yes…hello. I am looking for Dr. David Janus. Do you have his direct number?"

The operator said.

"Just a moment please. I do not show a direct number for a Dr. Janus. Wait a moment while I check for any new listings. Well…yes. There is a number for Aquatic Biological Labs, with a Dr. Janus as director, but no direct number for him. Do want the main number miss?"

Katie responded quickly.

"Yes. let me have that number please.

She dialed the number nervously. After several rings, a familiar voice answered with a business-like manner.

"You have reached the Aquatic Biological labs, No one is available to take your call right now, but if you leave your name, number with a brief message, someone will get back to you as soon as possible."

Katie said nervously. "Hello David…it's me, Katie. Please call me when you get this message."

California Coastline

Sidoo Tu soon learned that man-child ships could not navigate close to coastal regions. So, this became his new strategy. Safe passage meant staying near the landfall. He needed to avoid the danger of capture from more man-child ships while he continued his search for the good man-child.

With all of his kind now in the undersea sea, he was alone. It is a strange feeling. Sidoo shuddered to be the only whale in the upper ocean. Many man-child ships were everywhere searching for him. This was worse than he expected, realizing he is their only target. He needed to be cautious.

He kept trying to sense this new radio energy, but when he tried to connect with this radio energy, there was no effect and he received nothing in return. He concluded this must be the kind of radio energy Gandaloo Fah was talking about.

Now he looked to the other kind of transmission, what the man-child called am radio. The vibration was visceral to him. He kept sending a telepathic reach toward this signal. He could feel it had an influence on him as he tried to alter its content. '*This will make for good practice.*' He thought.

When he stopped his thoughts, the transmission stopped responding. He knew now what to do and what to look for.

Sidoo Tu swam all along the western coastline attempting to influence the am radio transmissions, but there was no response from the good man-child. Sidoo had counted on getting help from others in his search for the man-child. His determination became stronger. With his decisions solely his own, he realized this is not the right place to reach the man-child. In that moment, he felt a good feeling to swim to the Great Atlantic shelf. Sidoo was tired and hungry. The good feeling suggested greater chances to find this man-child and the hunger suppressed for the time being.

Meanwhile
San Diego Cypher Lab

Late one night, while deeply engrossed in the

analysis of a cypher, Katie made every attempt to find the illusive key to solving the problem. The code seemed random. No matter what logical combinations she applied, the pattern rejected all of her efforts. She was convinced it was not random, but logic seemed all together fruitless. Her concentration broke with the sound of the lab phone. The annoying sound jolted her out of her concentration. She wondered who could be calling so late.

She answered sharply.

"Cypher Lab."

A long silence urged her to hang up. Then she repeated.

"This is the cypher lab. Who is calling?" She demanded.

Then all of the tension left her body as David's voice emerged from the silence.

"Hello…is Dr. Kate Janus there? He said meekly.

Katie replied gleefully.

"Hi David…is that you? I'm so glad you returned my call."

David's continued silence showed little sign of

any emotion. The quality of his tone revealed he only sought to express an unresolved anger over her leaving him. Freshly bruised by his desire to retaliate she still hesitated…thinking better of it.

Katie ignoring his cold introduction replied softly.

"I heard about your recent success and wanted to congratulate you. You deserve it!"

David's gruffness, reduced by her response, replied friendlier.

"Awe… thanks. Well…He went on…I always felt if I barked loud and long enough someone would hear me."

Katie returned.

"That was something I always knew you possessed…great perseverance."

They both chuckled awkwardly.

Shifting the focus away from himself, he asked.

"So…how is it on the west coast? Are you happy now?"

Katie wanted to say yes, but mitigated her joy. She felt mixed to talk about herself. She suppressed her feelings in favor of encouraging support to David.

"I would love to hear about your new venture with the Navy. You must tell me about it sometime." She said, throwing down a gauntlet adorned with a subtle olive branch. Her invitation revealed a fishing expedition for any possibility for reconciliation.

David's social skills were not the best. He often missed these signals. He replied to her offer with a distinct indifference. Katie felt disappointed. Then with that failure, she began a slow retreat in her conversation.

Katie retorted.

"It is great to hear you are doing well now."

David responded in like kind.

"I'm glad to hear you are happy too."

She made one more attempt for an opening.

"So, if you ever get to the west coast, look me up. We'll have lunch."

David paused for a moment.

"Yeah sure…that would be great." He said rather coldly.

Then he offered an abrupt and unexpected closure.

"Well…you take care of yourself."

"Katie could not keep the sadness from creeping into her voice.

"I will…you too. Good luck with your new venture with the Navy."

David replied.

"Thanks again Katie…goodbye."

The loud click followed by the dial tone left an unspeakable emptiness. Tears welled up in her eyes. She sat there silent, wondering. *'Maybe she could've said more, or somehow different to encourage David more.'* Her mind reminded her of the proverbial image of two ships passing in the night. The distance between them seemed a greater gulf to cross.

David's call did not inspire hope, in fact, just the opposite! Katie's desire to mend things between them seemed impossible. Her warm feelings turned bitter.

The Next Day

Commander Straker appeared at Katie's office.
"Hey Kiddo…How is it going?
Katie looked up and smiled slightly.

"Okay I guess…it's this cypher. It's just been giving me fits." She exclaimed. She still felt wounded and disappointed from David's call. The cypher problem did not bother her as much as she claimed. She used it to hide her true feelings about David.

Straker could tell she was not her cheerful self. Rather than press her on it, he took a different tack.

"Listen…I have some boring but important Navy business to attend to this afternoon. I won't have a chance to grab lunch. So, why don't you join me for some early dinner at the club this evening. That will cheer you up…how about it?"

Katie hemmed and hawed…considering the leftovers in her refrigerator…meanwhile, Straker pressed for a positive response.

"Oh, come on…you've been putting in some late hours this week. You need a break. You can knock off early tonight…say around 6?"

Katie then nodded with a smile.

"Okay."

Commander Straker indicated a thumbs up and said.

"There's my girl." Then left the building.

Later, at an Unoccupied Apartment
Near Pier 14

Commander Straker arrived in a military vehicle, not Navy but Army issue as a covert cautionary action. He entered the empty apartment, with his adjutant in tow. He looked around.

"This will do." He declared.

Then he looked at his watch to confirm the expected arrival of the others. In the remaining group expected, three Navy seals and two Army rangers. This team of soldiers were highly trained 'seek and destroy' experts enjoying many forms of combat and insurgency training.

Soon, a black van arrived pulling into the adjacent alleyway. The driver exited and went to the rear to open the doors. Four soldiers, dressed in plain clothes offloaded one after the other. They entered the apartment unseen from the alley side entrance.

There, in the middle of the living quarters sat five empty wooden chairs. Four of the chairs were facing the fifth chair in a small semi-circular arrangement. The fifth chair sat next to a long demonstration table. Straker stood behind the table pulling the table closer to him. As the five soldiers took their seats, he pulled maps and papers from his briefcase then lifted the case, placing it on the table.

These operatives chosen by Straker, were experienced with many black ops' missions. Commander Straker hand-picked these people from whom he had served during other combat missions. These men he could trust because he knew they would die before revealing the true nature of any mission.

Straker envisioned in this whale gambit, an opportunity. It would provide financial security and a significant increase of political leverage and military influence.

Straker had a long-range plan. He met secretly before with members of the Chinese Proletariat, a general from North Korea, High level representatives from Iran and Syria, willing to pay handsomely for an opportunity to bid on the sale of the whale technology.

That was the easy part. The complicated part was acquiring the technology. His conundrum emerged in two parts. First, a whale is needed, a healthy specimen to obtain the secret knowledge of this water weapon. Second and most important, someone or someway to translate the whale language into ordinary English.

Straker knew his plan must include Janus. He is the key to the success of his plan. Dr. Janus will be able to interpret the language. He will do it with the aid of a computer program, very similar to the program devised to understand whale behavior.

Straker explained his plan to the group eager to listen.

He went on.

"This operation will be code named 'quicksilver.' You are to capture the whale specimen, take it to an undisclosed location and wait. When Dr. Janus succeeds to develop his new translation program, we will steal it from the lab, use it to extract the technology from the whale then proceed with the auction of both the program and the whale technology. The proceeds which I will divide amongst us all at the end, then each will go his own way."

Tommy Hardigan, a veteran of the Iraq conflict,

three tours in Afghanistan and a year with the Black Water Contractors performed many covert extractions raised a question.

Lukas Steel, the lead on the mission, granted Tom's comment. Commander Straker explained he would provide funding from a secret slush fund along with equipment and intel provided through a third world black-market procurement.

Tom leaned forward and inquired.

"How are they going to get into and out of a top-secret holding facility while extracting a 30,000-pound mammal in the process quietly, without arousing security? I don't mind getting into a firefight, but you want to do this in broad daylight!? I can't figure it, unless you've got some kind of cloaking device handy! And…no interference from the local law besides?"

Tommy went on.

"I'm sorry, but you're gonna have to convince me on this one!"

Straker looked him in the eye and inserted.

"I have this all worked out boys, to the last detail, believe me." He confirmed strongly.

Straker went on to explain.

I know when and where the whale will be taken. Once they capture it. I'm in charge of the holding facility. Besides, Dr. Janus' wife is working for me. I will convince her to return to her husband, track their progress, order a strike at the lab when the time is right.

Then Straker turned to Steel.

"Lukas, take Tom, Nick and rest of the team to the rendezvous point, use the old charts to find Shadow Island, several miles off the coast of Cuba.

"You can get them familiar with the layout for security and the holding facility."

Tom grinned slightly at Straker.

"Okay… Lieutenant sir!"

The group knew him as Lieutenant Commander Straker who led them in and out of many tough scrapes. They were loyal to the bitter end and would do whatever Straker asked. Straker closed by adding.

"This will be our meeting place from now on until we are ready."

The group left one at a time by separate transportation while Straker exited the front door toward his car, still waiting for him.

Later at the Officer's Club

Straker brought Katie to his favorite table. It was closer to the jazz band playing some of Benny Goodman's tunes.

After Straker assisted Katie to be seated, he ordered two martinis very dry.

He sat comfortably in his chair and began to stare at Katie adoringly.

Katie squirmed.

"Commander Straker, you are embarrassing me."

Straker responded in his defense.

"I'm admiring the beauty of one of the most attractive females on the base!"

Katie, catching up quickly, retorted.

"I'm more interested in food not romance!"

Then Straker responded with clever boldness.

"I can arrange them both actually." Now grinning broadly.

Katie noticeably blushed.

After dinner, they both polished off glasses of Champaign, and began drinking their second martini.

Katie could not stop giggling and started to slur some of her words.

"I cannot remember the last time I had this much fun!"

Straker looked at Katie and began his deception.

"Katie…I've been looking over your work and decided that you are actually not the right fit for this job.

Katie got tears in her eyes and reacted in utter shock.

"But you told me that I was doing great? Why are you changing your mind? Have I missed something here, I mean what the hell Commander!"

"The Naval Intelligence Department has looked at your credentials and found that your talents are under used! This didn't come from me, my dear. This came from my superiors! I personally love your work. They can and often do override some of my decisions.

"They are not firing you, on the contrary, it will be a promotion!"

Katie looked dazed and confused. She was

speechless for a few moments, trying desperately to understand.

Straker continued.

"The Navy has begun a new project, it's called 'Impact.' Quite frankly, they practically handpicked you from a number of top applicants for the job."

She struggled to get her poor alcohol-soaked brain to ask a question.

"So…she cautiously asked…what would I be doing at this job anyway?"

Straker smiled again.

"Why…doing exactly what you are doing now!"

Katie added."And where am I supposed to go for this new job?"

"This project is based out of Maryland, Bethesda I believe."

He made his message sound vague not to indicate his prior knowledge.

Straker didn't want to alert Katie so, as to make his proposal too obvious.

Deep inside the Marianas Trench, a narrow corridor of undersea mountains formed the supporting base for the Mariana islands. A large natural cave at the base of the larger of three mountains, spawned an opening into a rising reef ledge leading to a massive cavern.

The dull and murky blue-green waters of the Pacific Ocean flowed through and transformed beyond the great coral ledge leading to the opening. The dead coral left behind large clumps of sharp rocks which encrusted the reef over thousands of years. Around the rocks of dead coral lay buried several volcanic vents spewing forth heated water and dark minerals.

These vents warmed the clear blue waters of the undersea sea making this place a virtual paradise for the cetacean and dolphin species.

Shimmering golden light rippled through the azure surface straight to the sea floor. The dim golden hue radiated mainly from the roof of the cavern. The ceiling and walls glowed with a deep red-amber color, heated from the magma flowing behind them. The free trapped air above the sea was warm and balmy, matching the warm waters below.

Pods of bottlenose dolphins darted in and around the whales leaping from the surface performing a playful aquatic ballet. Thousands of whales filled the blue sea swimming around with complete peace and safety.

Around the landfall of the cavern several deep pockets carved out places where the dolphins could nestle, providing a good nesting place whenever necessary.

Simtah and Balen stayed close together waiting inside one such pocket for the magical moment of their first offling to emerge. Simtah was engorged with her new born, who recently became quite active.

Simtah was concerned she would birth before they reached the great undersea sea. On the way, Simtah telepathically asked her offling to wait a little longer if possible. They knew the offling was female.

They joined their tomes and decided to give her the name Lumah. Lumah's pushing intensified to escape the constricted space of her mother's womb. Clearly, she was ready to join their world.

Simtah and Balen expressed great joy with many pops and long strings of machine-gun like clicking. They thanked the Feyh for their blessing. Everyone celebrated the arrival of their new member to the whole family community with unmeasured expectation.

Then the moment arrived when Lumah's tail peeked out. It would be almost two hours later before Lumah would be free. Simtah's pregnancy was a long 15 months and she was eager to be free of the burden.

As Lumah's head finally emerged, the umbilical cord snapped and she immediately went toward the nipples to drink some of Simtah's milky paste.

Then Simtah and Balen joined their noses to commune with their tomes telepathically drawing Lumah close. A bright band of sparkling light arose from their tomes and began to swirl around Lumah. It appeared as a band of tiny stars now circling her whole body generating an elongated spiral. Lumah writhed within the spiral and wiggled her tail fin violently. This energetic exchange was the final gift from her parents for a long and fruitful life, given to all offlings at the birthing time.

All of the dolphins began to swim vigorously around the nesting place. Then with complete telepathic unison they leaped from the surface. Like a great chain reaction of movement, the surface of the sea churned, encouraging more to join in making the sea alive with joyful agitation.

Meanwhile
Bethesda Aquatic Laboratory

The lab filled with many cartons stacked around the center of the main room. Adjacent to the main room spanned a narrow bridge walkway suspended over a large seawater tank which, originally designed to house several dolphins for behavioral analysis, could easily be a holding tank for a medium sized humpback whale. In the main room, many of the containers contained scientific equipment, microscopes and powerful computers designed to crunch large amounts of data quickly.

David walked around opening the cartons. He methodically checked their content against his clipboard checklist. Several times he paused with his inventory work, scanning his new lab with a quiet sensation of pride and joy. His dream had finally come true.

Even with all of the equipment geared to support his theories, it wasn't enough. He obtained support staff from the Navy, but what he really needed was a topnotch cypher expert to help him with the algorithms. Katie would've been perfect for the job. He resolved to relinquish that part of his dream for someone less skilled.

He laid down the clipboard and removed his white lab jacket. He prepared to have some lunch at the base commissary. He skipped breakfast in favor of receiving his new 'toys' for the lab. He headed for the door and realized he left his keys on one of the lab counters.

When he returned to get his keys, the lab phone rang. It was the base gate. The guard declared.

"Hello…this is the base gate. Is this Dr. Janus?" The guard inquired.

David responded with a harried tone.

"Yes, this is Dr. Janus…what is it that you want?"

"Sir…You have a visitor here who is looking

for the Lab."

David seemed surprised.

"Really? …my assistants have all arrived I believe. But, it's all right. Let them in and give them directions to the lab."

"Okay…Doctor…I'll send them on their way." The guard confirmed.

David sat on one of the bench stools and waited to receive this mysterious stranger.

When Katie arrived at the lab entrance, she pushed the glass doors partially open and called out.

"Hello…Is anybody home?"

David heard her voice. Then reassured his mind he was imagining things. He got up from the stool and rounded the corner facing the entrance hallway to see Katie standing there, her suitcase in hand and backpack slung over her shoulder. They both stood silent starring at each other as if the other were a mirage. Then David spoke first.

"Katie? …What the hell!" He proclaimed with shock. Seeing her in person, he could hardly believe his eyes. Then the shock wore off.

Recovering quickly, he said.

"Don't get me wrong…I'm both amazed to see you and puzzled by your arrival."

Katie responded in like kind.

"I'm both surprised and pleased to see you too. When Commander Straker said I was to be reassigned, I had no idea it would be for you and your project. You know, he never mentioned your name. He only mentioned the name of the project…'Impact'…I think."

David smiled wryly.

"Yeah…well you know the military. They are not happy unless their projects have a clever and clandestine name…I guess it's for their record keeping, for tracking funds being allocated from congress."

"Well, David went on. I was just lamenting I have everything except a really good cypher… thinking of you of course…but now I have to admit my dreams have truly come to pass." David admitted dryly.

Then he added humbly.

"I'm glad you are here. In truth, I could've easily bungled this whole thing if I hadn't had your skills and expertise at my side. It must be a stroke of fate and heaven-sent luck to realize the good Dr. Katie Janus standing alongside working closely together. It was always my wish…you know. To work together on something like this."

Katie still held her luggage in her hand overwhelmed. She didn't know what to say. Yet, she very much wanted to reciprocate to his admonition of need for her. However, her memory of the telephone conversation echoed in her head. She responded with a mild defense against David's expectations.

For her, again, another total disregard for her feelings. Then, her rebellion reared its ugly head.

"Well…It was only my orders from the Navy that brought me here"

David's expression showed obvious disappointment. He frowned and recoiled from her statement. Then with further humility sprinkled with self-spite he responded.

"Well…I can understand! If you don't wish to work with me. I'm sure the Navy can find another place for someone of your obvious talent. Then David quickly added.

"I've behaved like a real ass…for that, I'm truly

sorry. But if you could reconsider…I will behave myself. I've done a lot of soul searching and can be different now… you'll see. If we both could try again, we could make it work."

Katie recanted her stiff posture.

"We'll see what happens. That's the most I can offer right now." She said flatly.

Meanwhile
The Sea of Cortez

Sidoo worked his way southbound and turned inward toward the Baha, along the landfall past Cabo near La Paz. His hunger made him less cognizant of the man-child ships in the area still hunting for a whale. The Eastern coast was still far from him. He needed to find food quickly.

He dove deep into the Sea of Cortez looking for his favorite food, but plankton was not to be found. So, he scooped mouthfuls of small tropical fish swimming in larger underwater tidepools mixed with fresh and saltwater near some coral beds.

He did not notice a small fishing boat parked several hundred yards from his location. The fishermen spotted what seemed to them a large school of fish nearby. The school of fish identified by their newly acquired fish finder.

They prepared their large nets as they began to troll toward Sidoo slowly and almost silently. The engine sounds from large trawlers provided Sidoo an early warning of danger. He could easily stay clear from hunters while on his long search. This time it was different. Suddenly dropping all around Sidoo was a web of fine knitted rope designed to haul in smaller fish from the water.

Sidoo caught within the clutches of the net bolted from his meal. He began to toss and writhe in the water. As he rolled and tossed, the net engaged him even more, making him desperate to escape. Sidoo kept thrashing about until his tail flipper emerged from the surface. Suddenly and violently Sidoo slapped the transom end of the boat hard, causing a lot of water to pour into the boat.

The captain became alarmed for the welfare of his boat and men. The crew thought they might be fighting a sea monster. They had never encountered a whale before. The fishing boat began to rock and move wildly in the water in all directions. This caused more water to pour in. Hearing his men screaming in fear, the captain believed the monster was trying to capsize the craft. Frightened, they were all about to die, he cut the net loose from its moorings on the ship's rails.

With one final lunge Sidoo shredded the net allowing him to break free of the strange web from above. He swam away with his heart beating wildly against his belly. After he swam a significant distance from that place, his body finally relaxed. Then he resumed his trek for open water to the south approaching Panama.

Sidoo wanted to reach the Atlantic shelf by way of the Caribbean, but he could not find an opening. He felt his time to find the good man-child was getting short. He did not want to traverse the lower most region of South America. Whales knew of that terrible place of violent sea. The place the man-child called Cape Horn. The waters there were quite violent even for man-child boats. This part of the voyage would make his task much harder. Perhaps, a greater risk and take a terrible toll on him.

He kept searching along the Central American landfall for any kind of opening.

He could hear very large sounds under the water. Sidoo emerged partly on the surface to see huge man-child boats appearing to crawl onto the landfall! This made no sense. Man-child boats are for water travel, not landfall travel. Intrigued by what he saw, his curiosity forced him to get closer. With greater caution, he moved in to get a better view.

These huge man-child boats were not interested in him at all. Their sides were too tall for man-child spears. Even more amazing, Now, he could see the large man-child boats entering a narrow stream that connected the two oceans. The Caribbean waters were within his grasp. He needed to join these large man-child boats and cross the stream.

He observed the boats carefully. They would begin to go and then stop, then go again and stop again. Sidoo was confused. He thought perhaps it was very difficult to cross this stream. Perhaps the man-child kept changing his mind. He continued to watch and focused his attention on one boat.

Relieved, he saw it finally cross the stream, but very slowly.

He reasoned, if he swam alongside one of these large man-child boats, he too could cross the stream to the Caribbean. He moved closer to one of the man-child boats just entering the stream and positioned himself alongside. Once he entered the stream he saw it was very narrow. If the man-child boat shifted too much on his side, Sidoo might be crushed.

One of the crew of the cargo ship stood alongside the railing having a cigarette and noticed their companion. He called out to one of his shipmates.

"Hey look!... He shouted. We have caught a whale in the canal." The sailors laughed at him and ignored his sighting.

It did not take long for Sidoo to understand the stop and go rhythm of the canal.After the cargo vessel eventually moved out of the last dock, Sidoo separated from the man-child boat and into the open Caribbean waters on his way to the Atlantic shelf

Bethesda Aquatic Lab

As the work at the lab proceeded, the tension between Katie and David subsided. Many of the cartons of equipment were emptied and the equipment strategically placed on the tables designated for certain analytical work. The computers were up and running, but two experienced some minor issues with the operating systems and had to be rebooted.

Some computers were simply for data crunching while two of the larger and faster computers had very sophisticated heuristic programs designed to process language algorithms, to seek correlations of ancient sub-tongues to mammal sounds.

The first task was to catalogue cetacean and dolphin sound patterns. The need to generate a comparison between known behaviors of both to the sounds they made before and after observed actions of each species.

Other computer programs involved visual displays of movements and being able to do side by side comparing of the movements via video editing.

Then David sat down with Katie. He began to explain the rudiments of his theories. In order for her to understand his approach regarding those patterns, he presented the results of his attempts to explore those proposed patterns during his field experiments and notes, which were all based on trial and error methods.

Katie needed a base line to model his theories into a code that would predict the results of his approach. Something he had not done before.

"Your field work…She declared…leaves much to be desired! It seems quite random to me. She went on…We have to be able to extract what you did along with any results you may have accomplished while in the water."

Then she admitted.

"I'm afraid that we may discover your approach and field work was for naught!"

David admitted to that possibility. Though the idea deflated his ego, he had to admit her suggestions may have merit. Then David had a euphony.

"You know, the Navy lost a submarine because

of what the whales produced. If we don't get anywhere with my work and this analysis, then maybe we need to approach the Navy, find out what they did with my ideas to help create that new sonar system. It suggests the strongest evidence and perhaps a solid place to start.

"I will get hold of Admiral Jainway. The Bright Eye project is a top-secret program, but Jainway may be able to grant us access to Dr. Collier's work on the project."

Pentagon
Admiral Jainway's Office

Jainway was on the phone with congressman Earl Hathaway, a member of the Ways and Means committee. He was negotiating to advance the next military appropriations bill coming up in the next session.

His secretary interrupted him on the intercom.

"Admiral… you have another call on line two from a Doctor Janus."

Admiral Jainway said.

"Sorry senator, can you hold for a moment?"

Then he pressed the button for line 2.

"Hello Dr. Janus. My time is short, but how can I help you son?"

"Admiral…Sorry to bother you but we need to talk. Do you have some time for us to meet?" David said.

The Admiral placed his hand over the mouthpiece and called out to his secretary on the intercom.

"Susan…be a dear and find some time for Dr. Janus to come in.

Then his secretary returned on the intercom.

"Well sir…you have some time on Thursday afternoon at 2pm.

Jainway then returned to Dr. Janus and inquired.

"Would Thursday at 2 be all right with you." David replied.

"Yes Admiral. That would be fine with me." The Admiral responded to David.

"Okay… I'll have my secretary set it up." Then he added again on the intercom.

"Susan…make an appointment for Dr. Janus on Thursday at 2 please.

Susan responded.

"Okay Admiral…consider it done."

Then the Admiral pressed the line one button.

"Okay senator Hathaway, where were we?"

Meanwhile

Bethesda Aquatic Lab

David re-entered the main part of the lab to greet Katie still browsing some of David's notes. She looked up and said.

"Well…what did the 'brass' say?'

David responded with a grin.

"We're good. I have an appointment with Jainway on Thursday."

Katie got up from her chair and walked over to the foot bridge extending over the empty dolphin tank.

"You know…We should have this tank filled with saltwater to be ready for one of the cetaceans to arrive."

David agreed.

"You're right. It was on my list but slipped my mind. I'll get right on it."

Katie went on.

"I feel we can't get a foothold unless we get that top-secret data from the Bright Eye project. I will continue in the meantime, to organize your notes and attempt to make sense of them!"

David frowned a little.

"Sorry…I took copious notes, but my organizational skills have always lacked a certain zeal."

Katie remarked.

"Yes… I know, my love. I was with you for five years remember? It's a miracle you have gotten this far really!"

David countered.

"Smart ass!"

Then Katie responded.

"Yes…I know."

Thursday 2pm
Admiral Jainway's Office

David waited impatiently on the walnut bench outside Jainway's office. It was 5 minutes past his appointment. He stood up about to knock on the outside office door when Susan appeared.

"The Admiral will see you now Doctor Janus."

David nodded. Jainway's secretary opened the inner door. Jainway shuffled some papers aside. Then looked at David and motioned for him to sit

Jainway explained the tardiness of their meeting.

"Sorry son, these senators are a frustrating bunch. The new military budget is up for discussion and they are back peddling as usual. Now…what can we do for my favorite scientist today?"

David began.

"Well sir…We have a problem establishing the link of the effects of my theories without knowing the full effects from the Navy's enhanced sonar system. What we need Admiral is access to that system, so we can establish a baseline for our research."

The Admiral squirmed in his chair. Son…you are asking for classified files.

The Navy has sealed those files since the incident. I don't think they'll take kindly to your meddling in their affaires. It's not just that those files are classified top-secret son…There is still an investigation going on. The Navy takes care of their own. This is their territory until further notice."

David responded with a strong plea.

"But sir…their investigation is linked to our investigations. It makes sense that we should share the data from the submarine's database!"

Admiral Jainway leaned back into his chair looking troubled.

"I get what you are saying son. It's just that the military are a proud bunch. They didn't like your idea that whales outsmarted them. You embarrassed them in that meeting at the pentagon. Remember, I told you then, you ruffled some feathers and they don't forget that easily. I'm sure they are busy trying to prove you wrong!

"To them, you are some smartass egghead from MIT Looking to make a name for yourself. You really think they'll be willing to help you further to rub their nose into the dirt?

"I'll do what I can, but those files are probably buried by now. I seriously doubt I'll have much of an influence. I can't promise you anything…but I will go to bat for you. You'll have to be patient… this may take a little time and an act of God to change their minds."

David left the Admiral's office depressed and hopeless, thinking his project will get sandbagged before it ever gets off the ground. He now began to suspect the worst. *'Maybe,* He thought …*his project was the Navy's way of shoving David under the bus, whitewashing the whole affair.*

David arrived at the lab late in the afternoon. Katie greeted him at the door.

She took one look and realized his meeting did not go well. She said sympathetically.

"I take it the Admiral was less than cooperative?"

David plopped his briefcase on the bench and sat at a stool nearby. His head dropped, eyes staring blankly at the floor. He wanted to scream, stomp his feet or throw something.

"I can't believe this is happening! I hate politics, the military and Washington!

They have all conspired against me…he ranted. It's all a plot to make a fool out of me and the work because I had the nerve to reveal that their expensive submarine was destroyed by some mammals in the sea."

Katie put her hand on his shoulder.

"Don't worry hon, it'll work out somehow." she said assuring him.

David shook his head.

"I never catch a break... ever!! He declared.

Katie looked at him and smiled.

"You silly man…I'm here, aren't I?"

Late at Night
Katie's Quarters

Katie dialed Commander Straker's home number. It was late, but she hoped he was not out lapping it up with his buddies at the club. After several rings, Straker answered.

"Straker" …he said in a gruff tone.

"Commander Straker…This is Dr. Janus calling."

Straker said chuckling.

"Hey girl…what happened, did you and your hubby have a spat?" He said sarcastically.

"No…but it's important." She said urgently.

"We have run into a stone wall. We are going to need the data from the submarine, specifically regarding the Bright Eye mission files and the…"

Commander Straker halted her.

"Whoa…girl. Back up a second. Those files are classified top-secret and the Navy has locked down anything to do with the mission."

Then Katie told him David went to see Admiral Jainway.

"He turned him away." She exclaimed.

"We cannot proceed Commander unless we can see the details of the sonar system and the modified algorithms utilized by Bright Eye."

Straker paused.

"All right…He said… Don't get your panties in an uproar, I'll see what I can do for my girl. By the way…you two getting along okay?"

Katie replied.

"It's okay… and we are working together just fine. Thanks for asking."

Straker responded.

"Okay…Good. I'll get back to you."

Straker hung up, sitting on his couch holding a glass of scotch. He sipped on it slowly and pensively. He considered this new wrinkle in his plan. He thought to himself. *'Damn it to hell. There is always some stupid curve I didn't count on. I'll have to make some calls when I get in tomorrow.* Then, he loosened his tie. The attractive brunette sitting next him began to unbutton his shirt. He turned to her.

"Okay. Now, where were we?"

The girl said softly.

"I remember distinctly, you promised me that drink.

Straker got up heading for the bar on the other side of the room. She held him back by his belt saying.

"Where are you going? We have some unfinished business, don't we?"

Then Straker turned off the light.

Office of Naval Intelligence

In the morning, at the intelligence office, Straker strolled into his office. On the way through the door, he turned to his secretary and barked.

"Get the Rear Admiral on the phone for me

sweetie…I have some business to discuss with him. As he started to close his door, he added. I'll be in my office."

He sat in front of his desk, then reached for the desk drawer on his right and pulled a bottle of scotch and a glass. he leaned back in his chair and mumbled under his breath looking fondly at the scotch… *'Ah, the hair of the dog that bit me, and another day at the races!'*

Straker's intercom buzzed and he responded. "Yes Millie…"

Millie responded.

Commander, the Rear Admiral is on the line for you sir."

"Thank you, Millie." He said in a kind voice as he punched line1 on his phone.

"Rear Admiral sir…Straker began…Thanks for taking my call. Listen, we have a small problem Sir. One of my research departments assigned to investigate the U.S.S Scorpion incident, has requested copies of the data from the sub and the research files for Bright Eye."

The Rear Admiral…paused. "Well, is this department you're referring to, vetted for top-secret clearance Commander?"

Straker replied quickly and confidently.

"Oh yes, Admiral sir…No problem there, I will personally vouch for the team sir."

The Rear Admiral paused with a sigh.

"All right…I'll have one of my adjutants hand carry the pouch to your office…and you'll have to sign for it Commander."

Commander Straker replied.

"Oh yes sir, absolutely sir."

Bethesda Aquatic Lab
Evening

Katie was making notes on top of David's notes for reference, trying make some sense of his experiments. She was tired and restless. The lab seemed very quiet…in fact, too quiet. She decided to turn on the radio for some relaxing music but the FM station was not giving her what she wanted. She switched to a local AM station. The announcer was talking with a band leader, Justin hayward from The Moody Blues, about his upcoming rock concert tour. Katie thought. *'Eh…I don't want to hear this crap!'*

Then she turned the dial to a higher channel which, now presented music more to her liking. The announcer began to speak of the next group, the Mamas and Papas, and their song. Then the announcer said an odd thing.

"I am looking for a man-child who favors the whales!"

Katie turned to stare at the radio…uttering.

"What did he just say?"

The musical lyrics continued,"Monday,

Monday, can't trust that day." …

Katie thought she was just tired and hearing things. But as the music continued,

The DJ, started to talk again about another group when he was interrupted again.

"Next, we want to play for you…Is the man-child who cares about the whales listening?" Then there was silence.

Now Katie went to the radio and picked it up, listening intently. Nothing more was said. She changed the dial to another station, then back again. Still nothing more was said. She thought.

'Oh boy, I've been working too hard!'

Katie continued to question her mental stability when David came into the room.

"Okay. He declared. The tank will be filled on Thursday."

Katie didn't respond.

David looked at her with concern.

"You okay sweetie?"

Katie started then paused…"Something weird just happened."

David's curiosity increased.

"What?" …He asked.

"Well…she started…I was listening to the radio and the DJ was interrupted, that is, he stopped in the middle of what he was saying. Then he suddenly changed. He stated this strange message. I wrote it down on this piece of paper."

Katie handed the paper to David. As David read it, his eyes widened. Then he looked up and grinned.

"This is a joke, right? I mean give me a break! …Really? He went on…You're pulling my leg!"

Katie shook her head…"No! She demanded… I'm not kidding. That's what I heard him say."

David sat down on the stool…and became pensive. He mumbled to himself.

"What the hell, he said, shaking his head… I mean, what's happening here?"

Then David began to grill Katie.

"Was this the only message?"

Katie paused.

"Well… there was another message before, but I ignored it thinking I didn't hear what was said correctly, or it was my imagination. But then…It happened again."

David grunted.

"Huh."

He kept going over her writing, again and again. He wrapped his hand against the paper.

"I can't believe this!... It has to be some sort of prank, don't you think?"

"Hon, I'm just as bewildered as you." She declared.

Then Katie explained.

"I even changed the station, thinking it was some kind of cross interference.

Then, when I turned back to the station, it sounded clear. But… for a moment, it was only silence!"

David was even more intrigued.

"Okay. Here is what we are going to do. I just happened to have in this box, a radio direction finder, I thought we could use it in the field. I will turn it on to that frequency, and leave it on. If it is a prankster, then we'll nail his ass."

Katie nodded in the affirmative.

Hours went by, the radio station continued its normal broadcast without incident. Now, it was late. Both Katie and David were getting sleepy. David was about to switch off the finder and close up shop. Then the station DJ, in the process of signing off, again changed his statement. "Sidoo Tu to the man-child…the one who cares for the whales… are you listening? We want to rendezvous and make contact"

The radio direction finder loop was spinning slowing trying to track the signal.

First, it rotated to the left…then paused and reversed direction. Then it moved from one position to another. David checked the coordinates. The first coordinate was in the middle of the city, but the second was centered somewhere offshore.

David concluded.

"Well…our prankster is either located in the city and hacking into the station with a pirate signal, or he is sitting offshore on a boat nearby with a pirate transmitter."

"Katie…he declared… Tomorrow we are going on a pirate expedition. The radio Station will be our first stop. Then, if that doesn't work, we'll contact the Coast Guard!"

AM 1095 Radio Station Next Day
San Diego

David and Katie entered the glass doors of the building. The station, a whitewashed small building pressed between two adjacent second floor apartments and tucked far back from the street, seemed obscure except for the bold 1095 AM logo pasted on the glass door and the transmitting antenna jutting high above.

Immediately inside, a semi-circular reception desk with a young man sporting a boldly printed flower shirt, a blond ponytail and a short beard sat casually behind.

The receptionist greeted David first.

"Hey dude, he said casually. Can I help you?" he continued smiling.

David thought to himself. *'Ah…a Hippy…that figures!'*

He wasted no time getting to the point.

"Hello…we heard some interference on your station yesterday. We wondered if we could speak with the DJ that was on last night at 6:30pm?

The receptionist commented.

"Yeah dude…well… that would be the Jackster, that is, Jack Wolf, we call him the 'Wolfman', but he left early yesterday. Said he wasn't feeling good. He hasn't called in yet. We have to get a fill in cause his next show is at 4:30 today."

David continued to pursue.

"What about your engineer, could we speak to him?"

The receptionist stared at David for a moment…Then responded.

"Yeah… dude…well that would be Eric. Eric was here yesterday running around. He tried to find some kind of transmitter problem… he said, maybe there could be some kind of frequency interference. I don't know really…Like I say, I'm not a techy. He only comes in if there is a problem or, when there is monthly maintenance needed."

David pressed further.

"So, do you have his telephone number handy?"

The receptionist continued.

"Sure, thing…dude… Here, He said, sliding the business card toward David with Eric's telephone number scribbled on the back.

"The only thing man…you might not be able get hold of him…you know, cause when he is not doing his techy thing, he's out surfing."

Then the receptionist added.

"Listen man…Eric sometimes picks up some weed for me when he's in Oceanbeach, not far from where he lives…just saying."

As David started to exit the glass doors with Katie in tow, the receptionist called out.

"Be cool dude…good luck finding Eric… man. And if you find him tell him that Jeffery could use some more weed."

David waved him off as they got into their car. David turned to Katie.

"Well…what do you think? Shall we try to chase this Eric guy down or, go back to the lab and continue to monitor that station. Maybe we'll order in some food…I'm starving, how about you?"

Bethesda Aquatic Lab
Evening

Katie switched on the radio while David turned the radio direction finder on.

The antenna began a slow rotation toward the radio station direction while Katie took sandwiches from the take-out and prepared a place at the bench, David began to observe the coordinates and wrote them down.

He watched the antenna carefully. This time the antenna stayed in the direction toward the radio broadcast and didn't move. Katie called out.

"Our banquet is served! Stop starring at the antenna. Don't worry, it will move if it picks up the that pirate again."

David nodded reluctantly, reaching over to take a bite out of his ham and cheese sandwich. Katie cut her sandwich in half and began. David looked at her and said.

"Aren't you hungry?"

Katie answered.

"I'll finish my other half later, not so much now."

Katie continued eating but developed a wrinkled brow.

"I just can't figure who would know about what we are doing here, I mean that message is really strange!"

David looked at her and shook his head.

"Yeah…you can say that again."

David finished his sandwich and looked over

the radio finder once more and Katie put the half
of her sandwich in the refrigerator. She turned to
see the antenna

Begin to oscillate.

"David Look, as she pointed to the finder
antenna. It's moving again."

As David went closer to watch, the radio
stopped playing music.

The mysterious voice broke over the silence.

"Calling for the good man-child who favors the
whales, are you listening. Sidoo Tu desires
contact." Then there was silence.

Katie and David looked at each other
bewildered. They starred at the radio in wonder.
Now the finder had rotated to another coordinate,
it was definitely offshore and making small
oscillations.

David jotted the coordinates on a small piece of
paper and jumped to the telephone.

"Operator, would you connect me with the
Coast Guard right away please."

The operator responded.

"Just a moment please. I'll connect you."

After several rings, Seaman first Class Gordan

answered.

"Coast Guard station 6, Seaman Gordan speaking."

David still starring at the antenna, explained.

"Seaman, this is Dr. David Janus at the Naval base in Bethesda. I have reason to believe someone is making a pirate broadcast off the coast near Baltimore . Can you confirm please."

Then the Seaman asked.

"Sir, can you specify the frequency?

David responded.

"Yes. It is 1095 Kilocycles."

Sir, that frequency is an AM band. Ship to shore frequencies are normally in the marine VHF band sir, between 156 to 174 megacycles. Are you sure about that frequency?"

David answered.

"Yes Seaman, I'm aware of normal marine transmission frequencies. This transmission must be piggybacked somehow onto a marine band. Can you confirm?"

The seaman replied.

"Well, I do not see any ship to shore traffic happening right now sir."

"Perhaps you should contact the FCC about this problem."

David looked disappointed and frustrated.

"All right, I will do that in the morning. Thank you, Seaman."

As David hung up the phone, the antenna continued to oscillate in the eastern direction, indicating a signal offshore. He sat on the stool and starred at Katie, baffled by what was happening. Then the radio started to play music again but again interrupted by silence and once again the strange message repeated through the DJ's voice.

"I am Sidoo Tu, reaching out telepathically through another, to contact the good man-child who favors the whales. We wish to rendezvous."

David got up and began to pace back and forth. *'It didn't make any sense really.'* He thought. Then he turned to Katie.

"What the hell is going on here?" He asked rhetorically.

Then the DJ's voice broke through again.

"Please focus your thoughts…with an answer, if you have heard my call."

Katie looked alarmed.

"Is this for real?" She said with tears welling up.

David looked at her sympathetically.

"I don't know hon. I'm not sure what is happening here."

The DJ's voice spoke oddly again.

"Please respond with your thoughts focused. I will be able to hear them."

David looked at Katie.

"Hey… David said desperately… let's play their silly game, we have nothing to lose right.?"

Katie's tears rolled freely down her face, nodding in agreement but feeling she needed some therapy now.

David coached.

"Okay…we'll do it together. Let's concentrate our thoughts to say, okay we hear you, can you read our thoughts now?"

"Yes, thank the Feyh, we can hear you now. We need to rendezvous at a secure location, it's urgent that we meet."

David coached again.

"Honey, let's ask where to meet.!"

Then the DJ's voice spoke again.

"We will meet with you, near the docking piers in the bay, on the next day, during the time of first darkness.

"Bring your receiving device, we will communicate with you directly, do you understand?"

David felt eager and excited about this wild adventure. Katie felt more concerned. This was really crazy. She didn't feel good about what was happening to them. She became suspicious and fantasized this might be a foreign agent or something trying to lure them for bad purposes.

Then Katie pleaded.

"You're not seriously thinking of doing this are you?"

David replied.

"Well…yes, actually. I aim to catch these bastards in the act. Land their butts in prison, it's a felony you know?... to hack transmissions like this."

Katie refrained.

"Well…I want to go on record here…This is not only crazy, but dangerous!

You don't really know what you are dealing

with, do you realize that?" She asked desperately.

David responded.

"Yeah…I realize it's a little dicey…but they heard our thoughts! I mean how is that possible?" He asked.

Then David said consoling her.

"We'll take Garret along with us, if that makes you feel any better. He's a muscled kind of guy that can provide back up in case we get into trouble and or things get a little rough."

Chesapeake Bay
Near the Cargo Docks

David, Katie and Garret arrive at the cargo docks at sunset. They brought the transistor radio held inside Katie's handbag. Garret was unaware of their purpose and sat down on a bench waiting for further instructions from them.

They stood by waiting for darkness to descend on them. Katie pulled the radio from her bag and switched it on, tuning it to 1095. The whole experience seemed preposterous to her at this point. She sat on the bench next to Garret fidgeting, feeling a growing sense of fear and trepidation in her gut.

David began to pace, back and forth looking out over the bay, expecting to see a small craft approach. He felt nervous as well, but wanted to show his confidence to Katie.

Then the radio went silent followed by the sound of static. Now the voice that spoke was not the DJ's voice. It was much lower in volume and tone.

"I am coming now… Thank you and thank the Feyh for your coming to meet with me."

Then then there was silence and intermittent static.

The voice spoke again and said.

"Turn your receiving device to the number 1096. This will make it easier to communicate."

David turned to Katie.

"Do it girl…Let's see what they have up their sleeve."

David continued to stare at the bay expecting a boat any minute. Then the water at the end of the dock began to ripple and enlarge. Soon a spout of water shot up near them. Sidoo Tu emerged.

David slowly walked to the edge of the pier and stared with disbelief.

He could not believe his eyes. There, laying on it's side, a humpback whale looking back at him.

David turned to Katie laughing nervously.

"Hon…he said…You got to come over here to see this."

Katie got up carrying the radio in her hand. She looked beyond the pier to confirm David's apparition. She too could see the impossible sight of the whale starring at both of them.

Garret stood up.

"Hey…what are you guys looking at?" He asked.

David turned to say.

"It's okay Garret, just stay there and sit down." He commanded.

Then the radio buzzed in her hand with more static.

"Please adjust the number to 1096 now."

Katie visibly shaking, adjusted the dial slightly.

The deep voice then said.

"I am Sidoo Tu, emissary from the cetacean population. I have come to negotiate a peace treaty with the man-child."

Now David's thoughts rolled out clearly.

'What peace treaty? Are we at war?' he thought.

Sidoo responded.

"We are not sure of the man-child's intentions. We regret the loss of your deep-water machine and the death of many man-child aboard. It is unfortunate that our offlings misunderstood your intentions and created a torqx against your great deep-water machine." Then more static sounded on the radio.

David entered into another thought.

'Are you referring to the submarine that was destroyed?' Then another thought immediately followed. *'This amazing!'*

Sidoo Tu responded.

"Our species is a peaceful species. Torqx is used only for great distance communications with other species. It is never used for such destructive purposes."

David was filled with awe and excitement. His dream to communicate with the whales had finally come true. He could not wait to offer another round of questions.

David sent another thought.

'So, this is how you communicate. What we call telepathy'

Sidoo answered over the radio.

"Yes, we call it communing with our tomes. We see that you make sounds

from your thoughts and are uneducated to use your tomes for such communications. This is why we need to communicate with you through your receiving device."

'So, you go by the name Sidoo?' David asked.

Sidoo responded to David.

"Yes. Sidoo Tu is the name of my tome."

David turned to Katie.

"Can you believe this is actually happening?"

Katie responded nervously.

"It's happening, but I feel I'm losing my grip on reality. I feel like we've been abducted by flying saucers or something!"

Then the deep voice broke on the radio, this time responding to Katie's thoughts.

"Do not be afraid the tome called Katie. We too have been concerned about the man-child's attitude toward the cetacean population, what is this 'flying saucer', a ship from the air-sky above?" Sidoo asked.

Katie was speechless for a moment. Then she giggled nervously.

'Well…she thought…It's what we talk about when we see strange lights in the sky. But they are not real!'

Sidoo Tu replied.

"We often see strange craft from the air-sky plunge into some areas of the sea, usually far south to the great icefall. We think they have a dwelling somewhere there."

Katie turned to David.

"Well that's what Admiral Bird mentioned in his expeditionary notes of the South Pole and then followed in his debriefings with Washington."

David went on further with his thoughts.

'Sidoo would you be willing to advance our knowledge of your kind. We have a special place where we could work together. It would be the first inter-species cooperative effort. It would help a great deal in smoothing the relations between us.'

Sidoo paused for a moment.

"Yes, we could allow this contact. Where is this place of special activity you speak about?"

David sent Sidoo a mental picture of the laboratory and the large tank filled with seawater.

Sidoo suddenly recoiled.

"Is it your intention to trap us in this holding place?"

David shocked at Sidoo's response of fear and suspicion, responded quickly.

'No Sidoo, it's not a trap! It is a large pool that you can swim freely, but also there is a gate that is open to the bay. You could come and go as you please. We would prefer that you could stay with us long enough while we make tests and enlarge our understanding of how you function, in particular, your communing ability as well as, this thing you do to control seawater. Is it like how dolphins control the seawater to stun fish for food, right?'

Sidoo relaxed and moved closer again.

He expressed a concern for feeding while in the pool.

"Our kind have to feed often, if we can. Can you make sure there will be food for me there? and he added…and your tome is called David, is that correct?"

David thought kindly.

'Oh yes, Sidoo. And we would be happy to make you comfortable and feed you as often as you would like…It will be safe for you while you are there.'

Sidoo made a siren of clicks and cries bobbing his head in and out of the water, indicating his willingness to trust the good man-child David.

Bethesda Aquatic Lab
Night

When Katie and David arrived back at the lab, Katie slumped into a deck lounge near the cross-bridge walkway facing the pool. David poured a drink for her then followed with another for himself.

She took a sip of the bourbon with her hands shaking badly. David took a sip and sat down next to her to console.

"I know…he said sympathetically…you are in a state of shock. I'm still reeling from tonight's adventure myself."

Katie started to cry.

"You know…I'm not so upset about the whale. I'm upset about how I've treated you, almost from the beginning. I thought you were crazy. Then, really felt you would give it up, but after five years, I convinced myself you were really unhinged. My father's words rang so loud in my ears and I believed him. Now…I just feel ashamed! I lost my faith in my husband…that's unforgivable!" She declared.

David lowered his head.

"Katie…It's not your fault. With all those hours and days, out there splashing around, whistling and banging on a drum, I'm surprised you didn't have me certified for a rubber suit!

"It was worse after you left. I went back out there, not because I believed. I went out there because I was angry. Angry you abandoned me, angry the Navy ignored me. Then I was angry with myself. I was embarrassed and a fool, in short, I gave up!"

"When the Pentagon subpoenaed me to testify, I planned to recuse myself, until I discovered during the hearing, my ideas did work but were stolen by DARPA and the Navy and they didn't tell me. They used my ideas for something bad. I was enraged that I gave up fighting for the truth."

Katie listened intently until her expression changed. She looked at the computer screens and her eyes widened. Then said in a serious tone.

"David, we can't keep talking to the whales with a transistor radio. If we go to the authorities with something like that, we'll both be carted off to the funny farm!

"After we figure out how to get Sidoo, or whatever his name is, into that tank somehow, we are going to have a hell of a job ahead of us, figuring out how we can develop an interspecies program, allowing us direct communications with these creatures. And please can we leave the DJ's out of it somehow."

David smiled.

"Yes dear, I believe you are right about that!"

Then David added.

"I think it's time to put away my toys and start fresh."

Katie nodded.

"Yep"!

The next day, Katie and David started to sort David's notes, trying to extract the rudiments of his theories he applied in the field. David admitted his methods were crude, given his previous budget concerns, not surprisingly but wholly inadequate.

While Katie formed some basic equations that suggested a heuristic approach to the language translation problem, David focused on equipping the saltwater tank with some sophisticated sensor devices and a rudimentary form of electro-encephalograph designed to read brainwave pulses, on a much larger scale suitable for attachment to Sidoo, the whale.

Since their contact with Sidoo was one sided, they needed to wait for an evening time for reception, the reception was just static on the radio at 1096 kilocycles. No Am radio station broadcasted on that particular frequency. Yet, Sidoo explained telepathically, during their last contact using the DJ announcer was more complicated to suppress his mind in order to control his speech.

Sidoo found that using David and Katie's joined mental efforts to focus their receptivity offered a much better chance of success.

David intended to instruct Sidoo on navigating the waters of the bay around to the gate entrance to the pool adjacent to the lab. To maintain a low profile, making the maneuver at nighttime would provide the secrecy needed.

Sidoo understood during his contact with Katie's mind the importance of creating a way for them to communicate beyond the sketchy telepathic connection he developed with them. The importance of this related to the transfer of more difficult concepts Sidoo wanted to share with them as well as, details regarding the secret operations by the military. Sidoo felt the military endangerment of the Cetaceans and Tursiops might suffer in the future was of the utmost importance to his kind. Though Sidoo expressed concern that this mechanical and electrical apparatus frightened him, he trusted their good intensions and believed in their goal of better inter-species relationship.

Now at 6:30pm David switched on the radio and turned the dial to 1096. They sat quietly in the lab close together calming their thoughts and excitement. The anticipation of further contact with the whale made them nervous. The hour past and the inordinate delay concerned David. Katie was more patient with waiting however, she quietly harbored some resistance to the outrageous situation they found themselves in. At 8:30pm both looked at each other as David kept monitoring his wristwatch wondering if their rendezvous was clear.

Now Katie wondered if they both had suffered from a hysterical response and all this was just a figment of their joint hallucinations.

David reached for the dial on the radio and turned the dial carefully back and forth slowly from 1095 to 1097 and back to 1096. The static remained consistent on all three positions. This made his heart sink into doubt. He turned to Katie and lamented.

"Do you think Sidoo changed his mind?

Katie shrugged her shoulders and responded.

"I don't know hon, maybe something happened to him."

Then David reached for the on-off switch and suddenly Katie held up her hand.

"Stop David!" She commanded. Then added.

"Quiet your mind and focus. She instructed… adding.

"I think I can feel something."

David felt curious to know.

"What is it?"

Katie responded.

"I don't know for sure, but I feel afraid, alarmed…or something."

David closed his eyes trying to feel what Katie felt. They were both silent for several moments then, a loud resounding thought emerged in their minds. It was Sidoo.

'Sorry for the delay…much trouble…a man-child boat spotted me in the bay. I needed to evade their pursuit so, I went to the bay entrance beyond the break water of rocks to hide deep below. When I felt they gave up, I returned to make contact.'

Then David sent a strong thought to Sidoo.

Sidoo, it is very important that we bring you to our pool for your safety now. Please… you must come to the gate now and we will let you in. Follow my thought to guide you. When You are near, blow the air from your blow hole so we know you are near, then we can open the gate.'

Sidoo responded.

'I understand you…man-child David. I think I am not far…based on your thoughts. Look for my signal soon.'

David turned to Katie.

"I will go now and make ready the gate."

Katie nodded.

David entered the cross-bridge walkway to the end. Behind the pool, there was a large metal gate hydraulically driven. The generator that powered the gate needed to be fired up. Diesel fueled the generator and it needed to be primed before ignition could be started, not unlike a diesel fueled automobile. David noted the fuel gauge was almost empty. He had no time to refill the fuel tank and hoped there would be enough fuel to drive the gate until Sidoo entered and then enough to close the gate after.

Soon, just outside in the bay, exploded a mixed stream of air and seawater looking like a miniature geyser. Sidoo gave the signal to open the gate.

David pressed the ignition, but the glow plugs were not quite ready. A Coast Guard Cutter cruising the bay, still in search of the whale, approached and slowed to a crawl. They switched on their powerful search light and scanned the docking area surrounding the lab.

Watching the fuel drop slightly on the gauge alarmed David. He ducked low to avoid attention from the cutter. Soon after, the cutter sped up and pulled away. David sent Sidoo a mental image of danger to stay submerged. Sidoo, already aware of the man-child ship heeded the warning from

David.

David stood up and glanced at the fuel gauge. The needle pointed to the red area indicating it was empty. He pressed the ignition button anyway. The generator started up. He sighed in relief as he pulled back the hydraulic lever to signal the gate to open. The gate offered a grinding sound and remained closed. David was desperate. He pushed the lever back and pulled it to the open position again. Again, there was a grinding sound and the gate still did not move.

David called out to Katie.

"Hon, get me the big torch from the cabinet in the lab quickly."

Katie yelled in response.

"Will do."

She came running, across the cross-bridge and to the platform where David stood. Then she asked.

"What's the matter?"

David grunted desperately.

"The frigging gate is stuck!" Then he took the torch and shined it on the gears below the water.

"Awe…hell. I see the problem." He

declared.

He turned to Katie.

"Hon, I need you to shine the light on the gear box, while I dive in and remove the debris."

Katie looked alarmed.

Feeling the danger in what he was about to do, she advised him.

"Please be careful, we wouldn't want you to be chewed up in those gears and become shark chum!"

David looked at her and smiled sheepishly.

"With all that seawater time I spent before, I don't believe I am going to be shark chum anytime soon."

David removed his shirt and did a swan dive into the tank channel.

David descended toward the gear box. He saw some seaweed caught inside the final gear teeth leading to the gate clamp. He pulled on the weed stalk but it wouldn't budge. He pulled again and again, the gear moved slightly but not enough to clear the stalk from the gear. Now, out of air, he ascended to the surface and gasped.

Katie looked on concerned.

"How is it going?"

David frowned.

"Not so good." Then he plunged below.

This time, David realized he needed some leverage. He placed his foot near the top of the gear wheel and pulled with all of his might. The stalk came lose and the gear began to turn. The edge of the gear teeth caught his deck shoe and pulled it in just before David managed to remove his foot. He watched in horror as he thought his shoe would block the gear again. The gear continued to turn grinding his shoe to a pulp. Watching the gate open with his last bit of air, he ascended.

"Got it!" He declared.

David climbed upon the platform relieved. They both watched with joy as Sidoo slipped through the gate entering the pool safely.

David reached for the gate lever. He pulled it back and as the gate began to close, the generator began to sputter.

"No! No!...not now, just give me 30 more seconds damn you!" He shouted.

The generator sputtered again, the gears moved

irregularly and kept pausing again and again. David then kicked the generator with a final furious blow. He jolted the remaining fuel still in the fuel line to allow the generator to run smoothly a few more seconds, just in time for the gate to completely close. Then the generator shut down.

David turned to Katie and hugged her.

"We did it, hon…we did it." He said with relief.

Katie then declared.

"You…my love, deserve a well-earned shot of bourbon."

The Next Day

David and Katie continued to prepare the equipment and sensors to begin their collecting and analyzing of data from Sidoo. Meanwhile, it allowed Sidoo time to get used to the pool's boundaries.

David draped the sensor array loosely attached to a make-shift net. He suspended it above so that Sidoo could rise to the surface allowing the net to cover his head. Several attempts later, all was in position. Then David said mentally.

'Okay Sidoo just relax, you may feel a slight tingling, but it won't harm you.'

Bethesda Aquatic Lab

The buzzer of the front door of lab rang loudly. The receptionist responded.

The Rear Admiral's adjutant appeared with a package under his arm. The large leather currier's satchel bulged with the package partially exposed.

The adjutant said.

"Excuse me mam…I have an express delivery for Dr. David Janus…for his eyes only."

The receptionist responded with a smile.

"Oh…that's okay, I can take that for him, he is inside the lab busy working right now."

The adjutant stood motionless not offering the satchel'

"Sorry mam…I am obliged to wait for Dr. Janus' signature"

The receptionist frowned and shrugged her shoulders.

"Very well, but he won't be happy when I disturb him." Then she turned to leave the adjutant by the door.

Moments later, David came to the door, with the receptionist in tow.

"I'm sorry Dr. Janus. This man insisted only you could sign for the package.!"

David busy signing his name on the adjutant's clip board, turned to Mildred.

"It's quite all right Mildred, I've been expecting this package. Then, in a pseudo-English accent said to her. 'You know, my dear…for my eyes only, top-secret and all that!'"

Mildred did not enjoy his humor, then looked disappointed declaring.

"I really don't like all this cloak and dagger business Dr. Janus"

David swiped his badge and re-entered the glass doors of the lab.

"Katie…Look what papa just brought home, compliments of Rear Admiral Cameron."

"Is that what I think it is?"

David responded.

"Yep!"

Katie returned.

"Okay, now we can really get down to business."

David pulled the package from the satchel wrapped in brown slick paper, stamped with bold red letters across the seal, 'Top-Secret.'

"Boy I can't wait to see what they did with my theories."

Katie retorted.

"And I can't wait to put some meat into these equations."

They unraveled the wrapping to expose thick documents and blueprints.

It was Christmas morning for David and Katie. Now they could begin to understand what happened to the U.S.S. Scorpion as well as, the mystery behind the whale assaults.

David spent the morning working with Sidoo adjusting the sensor positions and calibrating the array. He paused to watch her studying the mountain of texts and the blueprints. David offered.

"I can help you with those blueprints hon."

David looked at Katie with loving eyes. She turned and smiled. David went on.

"I realize now that my life was over when I thought I'd lost you. Working together like this was and is my only dream. I love you and need you hon."

Katie lowered her head.

"We got lost in our own need for self-assurance and admiration. We failed to uphold the importance of our joining David. Isn't ironic? The love of whales seemed to drive us apart but now, the love of whales has brought us back together.

"I remember now why I fell in love with you."

Then Katie shifted from the soft moment.

"Okay you nut, we can always be mushy together later. Right now, we need to figure out how we can talk to Sidoo. Perhaps we can bring this conversation to all the leaders, to the war mongers of the world. Let's do our best to change things here. Maybe we can stop the madness in our kind. The whales have brought us together, perhaps with their help, we can bring the world together."

David looked at her with tears in his eyes.

"Now…he said softly…I remember why I fell in love with you honey.

And you are absolutely correct, let's make this work, for us and for the world."

David energized the array. Sidoo jerked a little as he felt the tingling of the electrical energy penetrating his brain. David reassured Sidoo as he dipped his head a little. Then David sent a strong thought to Sidoo.

'Try to relax Sidoo, we want you to describe to us in your mind all about your kind. In this way, your thoughts will be monitored and recorded on our machines and the machines will guide us to the way we can bridge the language between us.'

In that moment, Sidoo thought of his home and life in the sea, the great undersea sea. He introduced the nature of their kind and the elder clan. Sidoo reached deep into his mind, revealed their home world, a water world at the rim of the galaxy.

Then he revealed their purpose on earth, even before the earth became earth and the world that was before, Tiamat. He revealed the beings on Tiamat, the Nom Lu Lu. He revealed the solar system's second star Ehter, the dwarf star and the planets that encircled it. Then Sidoo touched upon the early time when the man-child hunted their kind. Then he revealed the awful pain and destruction of Namoo and Lamoo from the black machine that screamed the awful siren.

Then he revealed the truth of Lahroo and Remtah and their defense against the deep water metal beast with the use of their ability to Torqx.

The computers began to decipher Sidoo's thought patterns. The screens scrolled on endlessly with countless streams of data. Katie sat back and watched intently and marveled at what they were doing. Then realized their task was just beginning.

'This challenge will be monumental.' She thought.

David again plied his thought to Sidoo with a question.

'Sidoo…he began…this thing you do with seawater, is it a weapon of some kind?'

Sidoo responded immediately with a resounding negative.

'No…Man-child David. We do not create destructive things…like weapons to make harm on other creatures…it is not within our being to cause destruction…we honor all life forms.'

David returned with another question.

'Sidoo…this thing you do…is it similar to what the dolphins do to collect fish for food?'

Sidoo paused for a moment to read David's

understanding about the dolphins and their use of sound to bring the water to cavitation. Then he replied.

'Not the same…man-child David. We call it torqx. It is not a weapon, it's a means where we can communicate for a very long distance, even across the oceans.

'The dolphins create a special acoustical pattern which when combined together in a circle, will converge and cause the seawater to suddenly expand. Even dolphins do not use their skill to harm, only to stun long enough to feed on what the pod needs to survive.'

David followed with another question.

'So Sidoo…what is the difference? The children from your kind used this influence on the seawater to cause great damage to the metal fish, which killed many man-children.'

Sidoo paused again. Then replied.

'Our kind feel great regret about what happened. The offlings are not allowed to torqx until they are mature. In this case, even the offlings meant no harm, only to chase the great metal beast away. They believed it was a monster come to hurt their parents.'

Then David posed the next question.

'Sidoo…how is this torqx created? If we understand it, perhaps we can show our kind why this is not a weapon, but a means to communicate.'

Sidoo paused again.

'Man-child David…if I show you how we do this, it must never be used to harm any of our kind or any of your kind…it must never become another weapon for your acts of war!'

David responded.

'I give you my word Sidoo…I will never let that happen.'

Sidoo began to show David how the whales use their upper cavities to produce a series of tones that create opposing tones the are both at one time complementary and dissonant, the combination begins at a molecular level and builds up a great twisting force in the water. That twisting force continues to extend for many leagues of distance until the point of origin connects with the point of destination, as though the two, were in the same place.

David sat down on the lounge chair, in

complete astonishment and declared.

"Oh my God…he blurted out… you guys have learned how to create a wormhole in the seawater. This is utterly fantastic!"

Sidoo began again. He revealed how these tones were created and what tonal frequencies were used along with their opposing patterns.

David then turned to Katie.

"Honey Sidoo just revealed to me the extraordinary science of wormhole creation. I mean… do you realize what this means? This could easily be adapted to the space-time continuum. With this knowledge, we could go to the stars, for Christ's sake, as easily as going to the neighborhood market!"

Katie then said with a calming tone.

"David…we must not get caught up in that! We need to break all this data down into forms we can manage, forms like heuristic equations we can develop into translation mechanisms between whales and humans."

Office of Naval Intelligence
San Diego

Straker sat in his black leather chair waiting for an important call from his spy working in the Aquatic lab.

The agent called on Straker's private untraceable radio phone.

"Commander…he began…I think the Doctor and Katie are getting close to a solution. Five nights ago, they brought in a whale and put it into the dolphin pool out back. They have been working really long hours lately and I cannot be sure, but like I said, I think they may be getting close to a solution."

Straker replied.

"Good work son. Maybe we need to get closer though with our surveillance. I plan to be there next week. I will bring along items to tap their phones and listen in on the ongoing lab work progress."

The agent replied.

"Very good sir. Will you be needing me for anything else?"

Straker replied.

"No…not really. You've done your part for now. Perhaps you should go to Shadow Island and lend a hand to help prepare for the arrival of our guest. I will take over now at the lab."

The agent responded.

"All right Commander, I will look forward to seeing you at the island sir."

Commander Straker leaned back in his chair after lowering his radio phone antenna.

He sat pensively for a moment. Then thought of a member of his team that could procure anything he needed for the mission.

Commander Straker received word from his agent. The code was established and already in the beta test mode. He knew the time of the assault was near. Straker perceived a simple plan. *'Strike, take the whale, take the codes and then take the female cypher in tow, as part of the backup plan when the woman becomes a hostage, then she can be used that way if needed.'*

No longer waiting for weeks or months without anything to show for it, Straker saw his chance and his feeling was… *'you reach for and take the opportunity to seize upon what you want.'*

So, in the style of his 'mission commander' image, Straker proceeded unflinchingly toward that goal, to be the winner of this game

There were many aspects about Commander Straker's gambit that made a normal snatching operation look like simple child's play. In this case, the details of his plan, though quite brilliant, possessed certain innate flaws that could've been exploited by others.

Knowing this fact impressed Straker with a certain urgency. All within his plan had to happen almost at once with incredible accuracy. In his experience, commanding troops under fire, he was willing to accept a certain percentage of losses in the process of winning.

Bethesda Aquatic Lab

Katie and David were busy compiling and programming all of the data they collected. Soon the computers would generate a perfect cypher to bridge the two languages. Then a new program would be created, using that cypher key to translate one language into another in real time. At the same time, the other language would also be translated in real time in the other direction. The perfect inter-species universal translator, the only one of its kind.

Straker walked into the lab unannounced. With the secretary out for lunch, no one was there to stop him. He casually browsed items in the outer office and found one inner lab door open, he entered. While everyone waited inside the computer room waiting for the results, Straker was strolling around planting listening devices in several unobvious places for later use. When Katie returned to the main lab and found Straker peering into one of the microscopes. She became perturbed.

"May I ask you what you are doing here? Not realizing who it was, she continued.

"This is a private military facility. You are tress passing inside a secure area, you had better leave before I call the base police and report you!"

Then Straker stood up and turned.

Katie stunned to see Commander Straker, became speechless. Then she began awkwardly.

"Commander Straker? …Oh, I'm so sorry, I didn't recognize you at first. She turned to see the front door open and declared …Looks like someone left the front door open." She went to close it however, she realized her misdirection would do little to defray the suspicion she felt, silently wondering why he didn't reveal his presence more openly. She went on.

"I'm sorry Commander. We are quite busy right now compiling data. I cannot stay to chat. I hope you can understand?"

Straker returned.

"No need to apologize Dr., I will leave you to

it" Just then his cell began to ring.

"Excuse me, I will need to take this call." He said abruptly. Katie left the lab and retreated quickly toward the computer room, hesitating in the hall. She paused to listen in on Straker's call.

"Straker here…he said in a low tone…Liam this is not a good time to talk."

"Sir, everything is ready. Have you finished planting the listening devices yet?"

Straker returned.

"Yes…he whispered…all are in place."

Liam confirmed.

"I have the receiver tuned and ready to track their movements. All is ready here sir."

"All right Liam. Straker said. Then he added.

Looks like they are ahead of schedule. They may have completed their work and are compiling the data and putting everything on tape. Tell Lukas, Operation Quicksilver is a go within 24 hours, have the team ready and the helicopter standing by."

Liam responded.

"Copy that sir."

Straker left the lab quietly without a farewell.

Katie re-entered the computer room harried. She put her hand on David's shoulder.

"We have to talk about our relationship!" She said in an urgent tone.

David said. "What? Can it wait, I need to load the second tapes?"

Katie put her fingers against her lips to signal not speaking.

"No…I'm upset with what you said to me last night!" Again, she signaled to David. Their conversation was no longer private.

David pointed to his office where they could speak but Katie shook her head against that idea. She pointed to the cross-bridge walkway. He nodded okay.

Once outside, Katie warned.

"David, I found Straker snooping around the lab before. I think he is up to something. I overheard him talking about some operation that was secret."

David looked at Katie compassionately.

"Hon, I think with all this going on, you've become a little paranoid. Straker helped us get the Bright Eye files, didn't he?"

Katie felt hurt that David wasn't listening.
"Yes. That is true but…well, I don't trust him!"
David continued.

"Listen, Straker is head of Naval Intelligence, he is probably running a number of clandestine operations, it's part of his job. I hear what you are saying, and I don't like the guy myself really, but that's not important now. We have what we need and we are very close to success. Now we have the proof, the evidence to make the Navy and the rest of the world sit up and take notice."

Katie argued further.

"Listen David, I love you for who and what you are, a brilliant scientist and pioneer, but you have always been a little naïve and far too trusting in people that do not have your best interests at heart!"

David quietly listened as Katie went on.

"Remember, you trusted the Navy, look what that got you! They took your ideas away from you without so much as a thank you. The University basically tolerated your ideas and allowed you to teach a few classes, all the while, they were laughing behind your back. Your so-called friends and colleagues belittled and humiliated you, even in public. Finally, even with our differences in the past, I always had your back!"

David responded.

"I know that honey. I appreciate that…really I do but, what about Admiral Jainway…He is responsible for all this that we have now. Isn't that proof of their change of heart?"

Katie countered.

"Don't you be fooled for one minute…Yes. Jainway made it possible for you to have all this and with the apparent accolades, but you must understand…all this is temporary."

David responded with dismay.

"What! What do you mean temporary?"

"Hon…she pleaded…we are being set up for a very big fall! All this looks great…granted. Then Katie added, starring at David fiercely. You don't get it do you? We are about to become lambs taken to the slaughter. Simply put, the Navy is looking for a scapegoat. They gave you this lab and all this equipment to give them exactly what they need, the evidence to go before congress for that all mighty increase in their military budget. Once they have what they want, all this… she said pointing in a sweeping motion with her hand… will disappear and the entire project will be sealed until the year 3500 ad!"

David looked down at Sidoo compassionately. He suddenly felt a sinking feeling in the pit of his stomach that she could be right.

"What are we going to do about this hon, if you are right?"

Katie straightened her lab coat, pulling it smartly together and looked at David squarely into his eyes.

"Honey, 'mama' is cooking up a plan to cover both our backsides. First, we'll begin by making copies of these tape reels, putting the copies away in a safe place known only by us!"

David smiled.

"Honey…he declared…I like this plan of yours already."

Then Katie perceived another idea for an additional precaution.

"David…I think we should code these tapes with a digital identification and location signal that can be triggered if someone gets hold of these tapes and tries to upload them onto to another computer. The coded signal will automatically contact Naval security first, then by weaving this code neatly underneath the clearance password, it will begin to send a beacon signal that will make the tapes act as a tracking device, providing longitude and latitude coordinates of their final destination."

David remarked sarcastically.

"Gee…You can do that? Hmm… I've decided it's a good idea to keep you around after all" He said with a wry smile.

Katie frowned.

"You know, I never realized you were such a chauvinist!" Then she smiled.

Meanwhile at Shadow Island
Off the Coast of Cuba

The five-members, comprising the operation quicksilver team, prepared their speedboat for the journey back to Key West. Waiting at a small airport near Boca Chica, a CH-53K King Stallion heavy lift helicopter would be standing by. The snatch and grab part of this operation was to occur at midnight for the whale transport to the Island. They would fly along the coast just under the radar ground control, to avoid or encounter any interference from authorities.

The high-speed craft was the type normally used to haul cigarettes, but mostly used by drug runners from ocean trawlers into Miami.

Liam's reputation to acquire anything they needed would often require the assistance and connections to crime syndicates. Those connections were plentiful in Miami. Anything was possible if one had the funds to pay. The stage was set and Straker's plan to strike was only hours away.

It was early evening by the time David and Katie completed the compiling, copying and coding of the tape reels. The original reels were locked in the lab safe. The copies, it was decided, Katie would deliver the tapes to a beach house owned by Katie's brother-in-law. The place would be locked, but she knew where they kept the keys. They were both exhausted and David argued that he should drive to the beach house. Katie insisted.

She knew the way and he would not find the keys easily.

The beach house was a perfect place to stash the reels. The abandoned beach house was boarded up from the last hurricane that struck the area and caused significant damage to one side of the building.

David went back to his quarters. On the way, he kept looking in the rear-view mirror noticing a black sedan following his movements. After making a second turn onto a side street, the sedan turned off heading in another direction.

He thought to himself.

'He wondered about his paranoia, his suspicion that someone was following must've rubbed off from Katie's rants earlier in the lab. I'm really not cut out for this spy cloak and dagger business anyway.' He laughed to himself saying."Relax, Dr. Janus."

Meanwhile, Katie arrived at the beach house. It was just after 9pm. The drive took longer than expected. Years had gone by since Katie's Brother kept pestering her to come and visit for a few days. She was tempted several times, especially when

she and David would have serious fights. The drive
to the beach house was long and thwarted her
lingering desire to get away.

Not finding the keys easily undermined her
confidence. The boat house was her destination,
but it was in shambles. *'Oh boy…this is going to
be fun.'* She thought.

The key search began simply enough but her
memory had become muddled over time. She
remembered a small metal box just under the deck
of the boathouse as far as she could recollect, but
the deck was pretty torn up. Then she worried that
it could've been washed away with the storm
surge.

She knelt down and began groping around in
the dark with her hands, moving the sand around.
Then, she felt the box. There… she could feel it,
but half buried. She pulled the box into plain sight
placing it in her lap, but it was so dark now. Not
much light from coming from the docks shown in
her direction. Still, she fumbled with the rusted
latch. There were two sets of keys, one opened the
side door to the damaged side while the other,
opened the rear door closer to the boat house.

She tried the key to the back door but the door would not open. It was wedged closed by debris inside. Then she thought. *'So much for that idea.'* Then she looked at the boat house admiringly. *'Now, there's an idea!* She thought. *I'll store the reels in the boathouse. They'll be safe enough after wrapping them in plastic.'*

After confirming the reels were secured, she got back into her car. She started the engine. Another wave of exhaustion rolled over her as she tried to embrace the long drive back to her quarters near the base. She said to herself, *'Katie…you can do this!'*

Bethesda Aquatic Lab
Midnight

Two black SUVs turn onto the street in front of the Lab. Slowing down, they switched off their headlights. Both pause in unison to confirm no one was around. The lab interior appeared dark. Only the lights outside illuminate portions of the parking lot.

The passenger window of the front SUV rolled down slightly. A Glock 9 mm pistol emerges slowly revealing the barrel of a silencer. Small muffled thuds tear through the night. A stream of bullets finds their mark, the parking lot lights. One by one their illumination is snuffed out quietly, leaving only the sound of breaking glass hitting the pavement. Afterwards, all was silent again. The team waited for a few moments to confirm the environment was still secure.

Three get out from the front vehicle followed by the other two emerging from the second vehicle. They all moved with precision, quietly removing their gear and approached the glass entry doors with determined purpose. One of the soldiers removed a diamond glass cutter from his bag. He mounted two suction pads on each door then inscribed a circle around each of the locked handles. After several rotations, the glass including the handles separated easily falling onto a soft pad below.

Once inside, Lukas contacted the helicopter pilot.

"Make your way along the bay toward Avalon Street and look for our signal, I will signal you with a search light. I will flash three times to identify the dock location."

The pilot responded.

"Copy that."

Liam and Tom jumped into the salt pool to place large straps around Sidoo. Sidoo was not alarmed by this and did not resist. Even though he did not recognize these two man-children, Sidoo concluded that the man-child David had arranged for this.

Soon, the helicopter came down over the dock lowering a winch cable. Lukas attached the large carabiner hook to the straps surrounding Sidoo. Lukas made a circular motion with his hand, indicating to the pilot he could raise the winch cable and lift Sidoo from the pool. Sidoo lifted from the water. Shock and confusion filled his tome once he left the water. In this experience, the feeling of exhilaration was absent. He loved to breach the surface from time to time. He wondered why the man-child David would want this, but he still trusted what was happening to him. The helicopter slowly turned with Sidoo hanging below, heading for Shadow Island.

Meanwhile, back at the lab, the team searched the lab for the documents and the tape reels. They wasted no time making a wreck of the place, turning everything upside down in the process. Then Liam discovered the safe located behind and under one of the computer tables.

Hardigan, being the expert on cracking safes, got right to work. He made several unsuccessful attempts to discover the combination. Lukas irritated by his lack of success, yelled at Tom.

"I thought you were good at that sort of thing!"

Tom retorted in his defense.

"It's a different model, I'm not used to this type of lock."

Lukas declared.

"Then blow it, for Christ's sake! Lukas demanded. Then went on. We brought C4 in case of something like that. Be quick about it, we are running behind schedule and the boss doesn't like to be late!"

Tom replied dutifully.

"Got it…copy that."

Tom planted C4 all around the lock tumblers and inserted the electronic trigger pin into the mashed explosive. Then he pushed several layers of blankets against the bomb to hide the noise while protecting himself and the others from possible fallout debris.

Tom then whispered loudly.

"Fire in the hole!"

The bomb exploded tearing the door half off its hinges. He retrieved the contents declaring.

"Okay boys, we have what we came for."

The rest of the team gathered the remains of their gear, stashing it quickly into their duffle bags. The team dashed through the glass doors except for Lukas, who paused briefly to confirm no evidence of their presence remained behind. Once outside, the rear doors of the second SUV flew open receiving the equipment bags now haphazardly thrown inside. The men entered their vehicles hastily and sped away quickly into the night.

Next Morning
Katie's Quarters

Katie awoke to the sound of her telephone ringing. It was David.

"Good morning sleepyhead." He said cheerfully.

Katie responded in a groggy voice.

"What time is it?" She said slowly.

David replied.

"Well… it's time to get up my love. It's 9am. So…David continued… how was the road trip to your brother's place last night?"

Katie sat up on her sofa, now more awake. Memory returned that she collapsed there, never making it to bed. Her back screamed with pain and stiffness from the unforgiving contour of the sofa. She said softly.

"Give me a minute…I have to make some coffee."

David said compassionately.

"No problem sweetie…take your time."

Katie left the speaker open on her phone, continuing to speak to David. He felt good about their decisions to make copies and hide one version.

"I think we ought to celebrate our accomplishments tonight with dinner."

Katie replied while pouring her coffee.

"Well, Dr. Janus, are you asking me out on a date?"

David responded chuckling.

"I suppose you're right. Now that we've added a new species to the family, I was thinking we could continue with that idea and work on adding one of our own to the family."

Katie paused to speak leaving an obvious silence. It prompted David to ask.

"Did you hear what I said?"

Katie then responded.

"Yes hon, I heard what you said. What brought this on?"

David hesitated to answer with a plausible reason, fearing she might not be receptive to his bold suggestion.

"Well, working together has made me consider the importance of our relationship, I mean staying together after this project is done."

Katie giggled a little.

"Ah…so you want something more than a date, eh? Are you looking to kiss and make up then?"

David recoiled defensively.

"Don't laugh, you are mocking my serious attempts to suggest a more permanent reconciliation. I was even thinking we could renew our wedding vows."

Katie sat sipping on her coffee at the table, slowly considering whether to continue to tease David more.

"So, you want to ply your amorous intentions on a girl who is still half awake?

That's not very fair. She said grinning and continued.

"Can we continue this discussion over dinner tonight. Such decisions should be dealt with over candlelight and wine, don't you think?"

David agreed.

Katie shifted the subject.

"I'm going to the lab early this morning to tidy up and remove the files from the server as a precaution, and I have a confession to make."

David replied.

"Okay. I will meet you there, but I have to swing by the base commissary to pick up some razors, toothpaste and some aftershave. I want to look my 'Sunday best' for tonight."

"Oh yes. Katie confirmed. I refuse to share food with a scruffy partner."

David followed her que.

"So, what's your confession about?"

Katie began.

"Well, last night that ominous feeling came over me again about Commander Straker. Fearing he might be up to something, I swapped the reels containing the data with blank reels in the safe. but I still took the real data to the backup location. Sorry, I didn't tell you."

David chuckled.

"Ah… my girl is rapidly becoming a sleuth as well as, a spy adding to your many talents! It's better to be cautious than sorry…right?"

Meanwhile
Shadow Island Lab 4:30am

The team offloaded their gear onto the dock of Shadow Island. In a single file, they climbed along the narrow pathway of steps illuminated only by their head band torches toward the lab perched high above. Liam went ahead to start the power generator. Then turned on the beacon lights to guide the approaching helicopter after firing up the computer equipment inside.

Minutes later, the helicopter arrived with Sidoo dangling in the straps. Lukas guided the chopper over the lab roof signaling to wait and hover as he activated two moving panels sliding open to expose the saltwater tank below. This tank was not a pool, but a long narrow channel with much tighter dimensions. Their intentions did not include a pleasant environment for the whale, in fact, quite the opposite. The channel was designed to keep Sidoo from moving around.

Once the whale was lowered into the channel,

Sidoo began to squirm and flap his tail fin vigorously. Now upset, he indicated strong displeasure with his new environment. Sidoo's feelings shifted to distrust while he wondered why the man-child David betrayed his trust. He thought perhaps the man-child David was angry with him and sought to punish him for some reason.

Lukas called Straker.

"Hello Lieutenant…The package has arrived safely and in place."

Straker responded.

"Good work. I have some details to tend to here. I will be along shortly. Did you bring the girl?"

Lukas paused…"No sir…we took the reels and documents from the safe and the lab was empty. We only focused on getting the whale out of there."

"Idiot!... you were supposed to go to her quarters. You have to go back now and pick up the girl! We will need her at the lab. While you are there, destroy the lab too. Make it look like an accident. Be sure you destroy all of the equipment, make sure Dr. Janus is caught in the fray as well. It will appear that foreign agents raided the place and killed him."

Lukas responded. "Copy that sir"

Bethesda Aquatic Lab
Early Morning

As Katie pulled into the parking lot of the lab, the tires revealed a distinctive crunch of broken glass. She exited the car complaining about kids throwing their empty bottles anywhere. Then she realized it was glass from the lamp above. Along the roof, she eyed the other lamps were also broken. Now she changed her mind, suspecting vandals at work during the night.

Hers eyes widen when she saw the front doors partially open with no handles! Alarm bells went off in her head as she desperately dialed David's phone.

All she got was David's message… 'You have reached Dr. David Janus'…please leave your name and a brief message…gritting her teeth, she hung up. Mumbling under her breath… *'Damn it David, did you turn off your phone again?'*

She entered the lab to see everything was turned upside down. Bench drawers on the floor and papers strewn everywhere…then she saw the safe. The door hanging with only one hinge still connecting. It was empty.

The burn marks revealed an explosion. As she turned around, she saw more scattered debris lying about. She darted into the computer room to see reels removed from tape drives lying on the table. She fired up the server and other computer equipment to see if files had been tampered with.

She began to rip files off the computers and server for deletion. She went around picking up loose papers and feeding them into the shredder. Then she thought of the satchel containing the top-secret files.

Fortunately, she forgot to put those files and documents into the safe the day before. She put them into her desk locked away temporarily. She ran to her desk and found it still locked. She let out a sigh of relief. She decided to try David again. This time he answered. She said.

"David…" Suddenly, her voice cut off. A folded cloth soaked in chloroform smothered her face.

She kicked and squirmed enough to let out a scream before she passed out.

David said with concern.

"Hon, you okay? He heard the scream and panicked.

He ran from the commissary jumping into his car. The engine refused to start. Several times he turned the ignition key and listened to the engine turn over while he tromped on the gas pedal. Finally, the engine roared and the car went tearing out of the parking area, clipping the front end of another car.

He was always careful with his driving. Katie would often chide him about being too cautious. This time was different. He threw caution to the winds. No one could stop him now. The car careened down the street narrowly missing on-coming cars while recklessly dodging other cars in front of him.

He finally arrived at the lab. Leaping from the car like a mad man, leaving the door swinging out wildly. He ran into the lab but found no sign of Katie. He screamed.

"Katie…Katie, where are you?" There was no

answer to his cry. He checked everywhere, but no Katie. Then he heard the sound of a helicopter above. He ran outside. He saw the copter moving quickly away and outward toward the bay. Thinking of Sidoo, he ran to the cross-bridge walkway. He stood, starring at the emptiness of the pool.

Tears welled into his eyes. Rage filled his heart. When he returned to the lab two men wearing camouflaged assault clothing and ski masks confronted him. His rage fueled the thought that something terrible happened to Katie.

He lunged at them, trying to fight with them. Their fighting skills far surpassed his meager attempts to overtake them and defend himself. Hardigan punched him in the stomach knocking the wind out of him. He fell to the floor wheezing and lost consciousness.

Hardigan turned to his compatriot and said.

"Well…Nick, that was easy! Okay. Let's get this party started. He pulled a canister of Sarin nerve gas from his bag and released the valve stem while he pulled his gas mask over his face. Nick pulled his mask over his face also as he dumped gasoline over the floor, onto equipment and tables, splashing the remaining fuel against the computers.

"That should do it" He declared. As he flipped his lighter into the room. Nick turned to watch the growing blaze. They both bolted out the front door, jumped into the SUV and sped away. They laughed when the propane tank supplying fuel for the coffee maker and single burner exploded.

Hardigan still laughing said…"Ah…Perfect!… Icing on the cake!"

Meanwhile at Shadow Island

Straker arrived to set up the prototype of Bright Eye next to the tank. He arranged hydro phones pointed at Sidoo. If the whale did not cooperate, he would use the Bright Eye signal to force a successful interrogation.

Straker loaded the reels onto the tape drives and began to download into the lab computer. It became clear, these reels were not what they wanted. Straker became angry with his men.

"Well, this is a real cluster fuck! You got the wrong reels!"

Lukas defended.

"Boss we took those reels from the safe. Why would they put empty reels into a safe?"

Straker grinned sardonically.

"Clearly, they were cleverer than you bozos!" Straker said.

"Well, when Hardigan and Nick return with the girl, we'll extract from her what we need. Then we'll connect with this beast soon enough."

Meanwhile back at the Bethesda Lab

The fire department arrived twenty minutes later. Flames still raged inside. The firemen wore their smoke inhalation masks and rushed in. The remaining sarin gas did not affect them right away. When one of the firemen spotted Dr. Janus lying on the floor he pulled off his mask and yelled.

"We have a man down in here!" …then he coughed and passed out.

Two more firemen came in after, saw the lone fireman without his mask on the floor and unconscious. The fire commander called on the others to keep their masks in place.

"Attention all members of the 48th station, there is possible contamination from a gas leak, keep your masks on tight."

They removed the bodies of the unconscious fireman and Dr. Janus onto gurneys, wheeling them outside. Next to the medical emergency vehicle, the medical team attached masks from oxygen tanks administering oxygen to the unconscious fireman. He slowly recovered, but continuing to cough.

The medical emergency team began to apply oxygen to Dr. Janus but he wasn't breathing.

Applying CPR didn't bring him around either. They removed the oxygen and turned to declare Janus deceased, when David suddenly sat up choking and coughing trying to breath. He desperately reached for his inhaler from his pocket. It wasn't there! Still gasping for air, he pointed to the lab holding his hand against his chest. The fire commander assessed quickly, Janus was an asthmatic.

The commander pointed to the two firemen unreeling firehose.

"Go back inside and look for his inhaler, it may be near where they found him."

Shortly after, they emerged with the inhaler in hand.

"We found it! They yelled.

David outstretched his hand taking the inhaler quickly from the fireman. He drew a deep breath then coughed deeply. With a raspy voice he said quietly.

"Thank you…you saved my life."

The fireman grinned.

"Glad to be of service…It's what we do sir." He said happily.

The fire commander approached David, sitting with a blanket over his shoulders, still coughing but breathing easier now with repeated inhaler injections.

The commander, a husky older man sporting a crewcut of snow-white hair starred at David. He managed a grin through his wrinkled face carved by many years of hard work and stress. He peered at him with deep blue-gray eyes and spoke to David softly.

"You able to talk son? ...Since you seem to be the only survivor next to one of my men, I have a few questions for you."

David nodded.

"You Navy people doing dangerous stuff in there?" The commander began.

David shook his head negatively.

"We do aquatic research only commander. Nothing really dangerous."

David trying to avoid revealing too much went on.

"Actually, the lab was burglarized, some classified materials taken. I caught them in the process when they attacked me and fled leaving a trail of damage to cover up their tracks. I will have to notify Naval Intelligence to investigate. That's all I know and can say right now."

The commander replied.

"Okay, I understand. I needed to ask for my records. Listen…He added… we found traces of some unknown gas present. It rendered one of my men unconscious upon contact. It might be lethal so, I don't recommend you go back in there just yet."

David responded.

"Don't worry, I won't, but I'll have the Navy clean it out. Thanks for your help commander."

The commander then yelled.

"All right men of the 48th, let's wrap this up, the fires are out. Put a police tape across the entrance."

The ladder truck pulled away with the medical emergency truck in tow.

David called Katie's phone again. He listened to her message, but it didn't reveal anything. He didn't know what to do next. The lab raided, blown up in fact, and Katie was missing. Still shaken, David needed to get his head straight. The Enlisted Men's Club was not far. He felt the bar might be pretty empty at this time and drinks were cheap enough during happy hour.

His car looked abandoned with the door still open.

David sat in his seat, closed the door and reached for the ignition. He gaped at the once beautiful lab he created, now in ashes, he thought.

'Hmm…maybe Katie was right? This whole thing smells of some kind of dark cover up! She might be in trouble…but where is she now? He put the car into reverse and confirmed his immediate plan. *I could use a drink…maybe two.'*

Meanwhile at Shadow Island

While in the port of Key West, the kidnappers dumped Katie's unconscious body neatly in the back of the speed boat. Katie's hands and feet were tied. Gaffer's tape slapped across her mouth in the event she awakened unexpectedly. Nick covered her body with a fishing tarp to conceal her presence from would-be nearby observers.

Hours later, the speed boat arrived at the bay of the island. While Hardigan moored the boat to the dock, Nick pulled the tarp back, grabbed Katie's body and slung her body over his shoulder like a side of beef.

In the lab, Straker and the other members of the team worked to prepare for the extraction process. When Nick entered he said coldly.

"Okay Lieutenant, where do you want the woman?

Straker replied.

"Untie her… remove the tape from her mouth and place her over there…he said pointing to the nearby couch. We'll leave her there until she wakes up. We'll give her time to rest. She needs to be able to talk later.

"Are you sure you want me to untie her now… sir? Nick said concerned.

"It's okay! Where is she going to go? It's a long swim to Key West!" Straker commented with a sardonic smile.

Meanwhile at the Enlisted Men's Club

As David entered the club, the only person present was the bartender polishing glasses. The bartender looked up and said.

"Good morning…as you can see there are plenty of seats, take your pick."

David replied.

I'm not hungry…I'll just sit at the bar for liquid lunch… thanks."

David focused on the night before, leading into the morning incident over his second shot of bourbon. He tried to recall Katie's exact words. His thoughts still muddled from his altercation. His concern for Katie's welfare and whereabouts crowded any other thoughts.

His mind drifted to the missing tapes. He struggled to remember her words.

She mentioned something about swapping out the data tapes for blank tapes. The bourbon began to have an effect then his memory became clear. She added some sort of way to make the tapes function as a tracer.

Then he jumped from the bar seat, slammed a fifty-dollar bill on the bar…exclaiming.

"Maybe I can find her…"

David darted toward the door.

The bartender looked up to see the bar door

swinging closed, but replied a little late.

"What did you say?"

No one was there to reply.

Feeling desperate, David drove through the streets ignoring his usual cautionary driving habits. When he arrived at the lab, nothing had changed… It was still in shambles. He ducked under the police line of yellow tape and entered the partially open doors to the lab.

All of the lab computers suffered from extreme fire damage. Then he thought of Katie's office. He might be able to access what he wanted from her laptop. The door was locked and he had no key. He thought.

'Well…I have no choice but to break the glass… hell…what's one more burglary!'

He wrapped his coat around his arm pushing his elbow violently into the door. The glass didn't break as he expected. The safety glass prevented a clean break. After several attempts, a crack appeared. Repeated assaults brought success. The glass pane separated enough to reach the handle inside.

He went quickly to her closed laptop. He

suddenly realized he didn't have her password. He tried several combinations without success. He stopped to ponder what password she might have used.

Her birthday didn't work, her mother's address didn't work either. His mind now frantic for an answer he screamed in anger. After a moment, he had a hunch. He punched in the date of their anniversary…There it was, he was in!

'*Thank God*…he thought grinning…*that she considered their anniversary as a password.*'

The file directory revealed both sets of tapes and the tracer code. He separated the code, so only the trigger for the tracer signal and not the Naval Police was activated.

He set the GPS application on her computer to track the signal. He waited impatiently for the computer to triangulate the signal source. The coordinates pointed to a location south of the Keys, near Cuba.

He thought, *Cuba?* Then he jotted down the longitude and latitude. He put the coordinates back into the computer to find the exact location…It was an island off the coast of Cuba, an island called Shadow Island.

David returned to his car. The gas tank was very low. He realized he would not make it to Key West without refueling and he would need to hire a boat once there. These guys who roughed him up, destroyed his lab and kidnapped Katie were definitely professionals, not amateurs. He imagined they maybe military contractors, in fact. David thought twice about barging in to save the day all alone. He needed a plan.

Meanwhile at Shadow Island

Katie awakened. Her head ached from the effects of the chloroform. She looked around to get her bearings then Commander Straker loomed into view.

She confronted Straker.

"What the hell is going on Commander? Why am I here sir against my will?"

Straker replied.

"Well Dr. Janus you are here to assist in the continuation of your experiments with the whales."

Katie replied strongly.

"I will report you to the FBI, NSA and CIA if you do not release me this instant!"

Straker retorted.

"Really…Dr. Janus?... You surprise me, I thought you were an intelligent woman…He said with a grimace. You are not in any position to cast threats to me. You are being detained on my orders for suspicion of espionage with foreign agents. You are under house arrest."

Lukas entered the room and declared.

"Everything is ready sir…the whale is mildly sedated and ready for interrogation sir."

Katie stood up with eyes widened with horror. She looked beyond Lukas. She saw the outer walls of Sidoo's tank feeling fury raging through her body. She went to the tank and looked down at Sidoo. Sidoo rolled a little to look at her with a whimpering series of clicks. She broke into tears feeling helpless. Silently, she transmitted her thoughts of sorrow at Sidoo's dilemma and fate.

Sidoo nodded his head acknowledging her feelings. Now Sidoo knew this was not the man-child David's doing.

Then Nick switched on the Bright Eye

equipment and lowered the hydrophones into the water. Straker engaged the signal strong enough to cause pain but not lethal. Sidoo writhed and splashed his tail fin vigorously.

Katie screamed.

"Stop it…stop it!" She demanded.

Straker disengaged Bright Eye then turned to Katie.

"I know you deliberately switched out the tape reels containing the code and put blank reels in the safe. Very clever girl…So now you have a choice. Tell me what I need to know about the whale's saltwater weapon, or I will continue to torture the beast until you comply."

Katie sobbing deeply did not answer. The Straker administered the signal again but the signal strength was stronger.

Sidoo thrashed about in the tank but the space was too small for the whale to wiggle free. Katie screamed again.

"Stop…please stop…you are going to kill him with that infernal machine!"

Straker repeated his demand.

"Okay… I will stop but, you must comply with

my request."

Meanwhile Key West Port

David arrived in Key West just after dark. He needed a boat, a fast boat. The marina was closed and the gate locked for the night. The night guard was walking away from the gate just as David approached.

"Sir… I need the fastest boat available tonight." …He said urgently.

The guard looked at him sorrowfully.

"Sir…The marina is closed for the night…I can't help you. Come back in the morning, you should be able to find someone to help you then."

David pleaded.

"You don't understand. It's a matter of life and death…I must get a fast boat as soon as possible."

The guard laughed.

"You're kidding right…did that rat-bastard Jake put you up to this?"

David reeled back.

"What…No, who the hell is Jake?"

David repeated his demand.

"Please…you must help me…My wife has been kidnapped and I have to find her before it's too late! …Please."

Shadow Island Lab

In spite of Straker's demands, Katie was at a disadvantage. The best she could offer was to use her memory recall of the experiments in the Bethesda lab.

Continued torture of Sidoo pressed her into submission. She could not or would not reveal Sidoo's explanation of the torqx technology. She tried her best to stall.

She began by revealing some of Sidoo's language format. She told Straker that the main form of communication between cetaceans is primarily telepathic. She felt the information would buy her more time, remembering that even though the tape reels were essentially empty of any real data, the encoded tracer signal remained her secret and hope. Ultimately, both her and Sidoo would be rescued. In addition to that thought, she wanted Commander Straker hung out to dry for his traitorous actions.

Katie also suspected that once Straker could eliminate his need of her knowledge, he could then extract what he wanted directly from Sidoo. Katie acutely aware of this situation, her life would be expendable and given Straker's obvious determination and ruthlessness, her demise would be a probable certainty.

Using a white board to outline a translation strategy, she wrote down key elements that were transposed incorrectly purposely, figuring that Straker would not catch on to her devious maneuver. For some time Straker accepted her explanations but he was no fool and all the while suspected she might be stalling.

She knew her explanations could not be tested without the apparatus to connect to Sidoo's brain neurons. Her algorithms for dual real time translation between two species remained only in her mind. She purposely left out the final keys, which depended on the correct organization of the heuristic elements.

Even though Straker's knowledge of heuristic coding was limited and that would be her advantage. However, if he realized during her explanations, the dual algorithms would be a logical conclusion, her plan to stall could fall apart. She also realized that Commander Straker, a battle tested field commander and logical analysis his forte would be his ally and his power to scrutinize her devious approach.

After several hours, Katie declared her memory devoid of any further information. As suspected, Commander Straker's analysis of her data initiated several questions. Straker began.

"Dr. Janus, I'm not clear as to how to proceed. Your data presented has many holes missing."

Katie replied.

"That's all I can remember."

Straker not satisfied with her answer, turned on Bright Eye again and applied the signal to Sidoo. Katie protested strongly appealing to Straker's common sense.

"If you keep torturing the whale, he may die on you and all the data in the world will not help you get what you want!"

Straker retorted.

"That may be true, but if I don't get what I want, I assure you you'll be the next victim!"

Straker stopped torturing Sidoo and posed his next question.

"Given you have provided the codex to

cetacean language translation, and knowing that I, or anyone else cannot mentally connect to the beast, how on God's green earth are these code patterns utilized in some practical way?"

Katie responded smugly.

"You will need a transponder to connect the whale's mind to your mind. I do not see anything like that which could accomplish that transposition in this lab."

Straker intrigued by her obvious posturing inquired.

"So, what kind of equipment is needed to function as a transponder?

"An electroencephalograph! ...an apparatus large enough to reach the cerebral cortex of the whale's mind yet small enough for your puny brain!"

Straker looked at her puzzled.

"Well thank you for that. As it turns out, the Navy developed a magnetic interface developed for the CIA's MK Ultra program. It's an advanced array originally designed to alter mental constructs or simply put, a form of 'mind control' for their top-secret super soldier program. And…we just happened to have that equipment in this lab, previously utilized for that purpose."

Katie shocked about this revelation, became speechless. Now she felt cornered. She quickly surmised he would require her to reconfigure the array to work with her codex. Once she completed the reconfiguration, he could realize that the codex she provided was incorrectly sequenced.

Straker commenced.

"Okay, miss cypher expert… you will begin to make the necessary changes on the magnetic interface."

Katie balked saying.

"My codex works with an electrical interface, not magnetic. My codex would have to be altered to become compatible with the magnetic probes. That's a very big deal!"

Straker retorted.

"Well, I suggest you get to it my dear, or the beauty will surely die with her beast."

Katie declared.

"Okay…But no more torture, or you won't get your precious interface conversion from me."

"Agreed…However, I do not make idle threats

my dear, so be sure your actions are without any further delays or distractions…and should you stray, I assure you what I have planned for you, before your demise, will make you beg to end your meaningless existence." Straker warned.

Meanwhile at the Key West Pier

The pier guard told David.

"I cannot guarantee anything mind you, but I will make a couple of calls, wait here."

David nodded.

The delays encountered so far increased his agony of not doing enough. He prayed that he would get cooperation and soon. Time was of the essence. Soon the guard returned.

"I have good news and bad news. I called the owners of the two fastest boats moored at the marina. One answered with a message while, the other is on vacation in Morocco. We'll have to wait and see if Mr. Hassim calls back."

David continued his plea.

"When and if he calls back, please tell him I want to hire his boat and price is no object… also make sure he knows someone's life is on the line. Please tell him this is most urgent."

Caleb Hassim's radio phone sound was turned off. He intended there would be no interruptions of his plans for a private party given to a few close friends at his villa in Key largo, now in full swing.

Two hours passed and still no returned call from Hassim. David's concern was turning into full blown madness. He kept bothering the night guard every 15 minutes for any news.

As Hassim bid a good night to the last of his friends, he entered his luxurious bedroom and sat on his bed, loosening his tie and opening his tuxedo jacket buttons. The champagne and occasional sharing of hard drinks with his close friends and business associates left him with a strong buzz. He thought of taking a shower before bed. He removed his jacket and placed it over a chair next to his desk. As he methodically removed his tie clip and diamond cuff links, he noticed his phone flashing with a message from the pier in Key West.

Thinking there might be a problem with his boat, he returned the guard's call.

"Telly…What's going on? It's pretty late for your call. Is there anything wrong at the slip?"

The guard began with an exaggerated apology and then he explained the situation.

Hassim began.

"Okay who is this guy…do you know him?"

Telly responded.

"Well no, but he is some sort of doctor I guess and connected to the US Navy."

Hassim became hesitant.

"When does he want to use my boat?

Telly replied.

"Actually, he is saying it's urgent…a matter of life and death. He wants to rent it now!"

Hassim wondered. *Is this guy on the run from some authority or drugs?* Then he asked further.

"Does this guy look legitimate…I mean can he afford my price should I agree?"

Telly paused…then replied.

"Hassim he is standing near me…he is dress well…do you wish to speak to him?"

Hassim answered immediately.

"Yes. Put him on."

David pleaded quickly.

"Hello…This is Dr. David Janus. Some very bad men have kidnapped my wife. I have intel strongly suggesting they have taken her to an island off the coast of Cuba, called Shadow Island. I think her life is in mortal danger.

"These guys are ruthless and dangerous. That's why I need a very fast boat… right away sir." Your boat is my only chance to save her…please, will you help me?"

Hassim paused…then replied.

"That's quite a trip from Key West…my boat will need to be fueled. This is going to cost you my friend…I hope you have the means to pay for it?"

David replied.

"Look, money is no object…I will pay you what ever you want…will you do it?"

Hassim said.

"Put the guard back on the phone."

"Telly…Gas up my boat. I'll be there in an hour or so."

Telly replied.

"Okay Mr. Hassim…right away sir."

Telly hung up and turned to David.

"Okay you are in luck. Mr. Hassim is coming."

David inquired with desperation.

"Soon…he said. He is coming from his villa in Key Largo. In the meantime, I will need to fill his tanks…it's a long journey from here. Sit tight he'll get here soon."

An hour and twenty minutes later, a silver Mercedes convertible pulled up to the pier and parked near the slip. The guard had just finished refueling his speedboat. Hassim got out and shook the hand of the guard and confirmed the refueling complete. Then he walked over to David.

"So…you are the desperate man looking to save his wife from peril? I am Celeb Hassim." shoving his hand beyond his long gray cashmere top coat to greet David.

David said immediately.

"Hello…glad to meet you and thank you so much for your kind offer, in the middle of the night."

David shook his hand and said."Can we go now please?"

Hassim the chided.

"Perhaps, you will not be so pleased when I tell you what this trip is going to cost you tonight!"

David paused for a moment.

"Okay what will you charge me for this excursion?"

Hassim delayed his answer. Then he looked David in the eye and said.

"I will need to be charging you for the extra fuel and the wear and tear on my pride and joy. It will cost you 10,000 dollars round trip payable in US dollars cash."

David paused to speak.

"Are you kidding?"

Hassim smiled.

"I told you it would be expensive. Are we a go, or not?"

David responded.

"Well, you have me at a disadvantage, but I have no choice under the circumstances. I only have half on me, but it's only a one-way journey."

Hassim replied.

"Well maybe it's a one-way journey for you my friend, but the journey for me is still round-trip, so the offer is the same."

I will accept the 5,000 as a down payment and when you return, you will give me the rest. But. In case you renege, you will give me your driving license as collateral, this way I know where you live…got it?"

David relented.

"All right…you have a deal." Then he handed over his license and continued his refrain.

"Now…can we leave please. By the way, how fast is your boat?"

Hassim turned to David.

"Cast off the mooring line, will you?"

When the 4 inboard engines of the speedboat began to growl and Hassim turned the wheel and headed for the open ocean he replied.

"My friends race my boat many times, the fastest time was compared to land travel at 102 miles per hour. I hope that is fast enough for you?"

David replied glibly.

"That will do…Thanks…How long will it take for us to get there?"

Hassim replied.

"At full throttle, I would expect about 1 hour and 30 minutes."

David sighed.

"Great!"

Hassim sat in the pilot's seat keeping one hand on the wheel and the other on the throttle. David sat in back next to the transom watching forward with an occasional splash of seawater hitting him in the face. Fear grabbed his stomach as the bow of the boat repeatedly leapt out of the ocean skimming the water like a flying fish. He had never experienced anything like this before. He thought many times along the way, how terrifying this ride can be. It was more out of the water than in it.

The noise of the engines and the roar of quaking waves bouncing off the bow made it almost impossible to converse without shouting. David decided to move closer to the front of the boat, in order to coach Hassim on the approach maneuver.

"When we get close to the island, let's circle the whole island with low speed so as to not arouse suspicion. When I am satisfied which side to approach, I will let you know. You won't have to moor your boat, I will jump in and swim the rest of the way."

Hassim looked at David incredulously.

"Well, if you say so…it's your funeral. These waters are known to be pretty rough. I hope you are a good swimmer?"

David nodded.

"I've spent a lot of time in the ocean water, I'll be okay."

The Shadow lab complex was built on the highest point of the island. This was a high security installation, designed to give residents a full view of the entire coastline. The CIA went to extreme trouble making sure they could maintain a constant vigilance to any oncoming intruders. In this case, however, the CIA abandoned this location many years ago, when the MK Ultra program was disbanded. David would have an even chance of approaching without being spotted.

Shadow Island complex

Hassim continued past Cuba. It was 4:05 am. The island known as Shadow loomed into view. David turned to Hassim.

"Best we approach the island slowly. We don't want to awaken the sleeping dog too early."

Hassim nodded in agreement. He slowed the boat by cutting off the two inboard engines cutting their noise in half. He moved in at a mere crawl compared to their high-speed approach. As David instructed, Hassim began a slow circle about the island. There were only lights illuminating the stairs ascending the lab complex other than one section of the lab where the interrogation continued.

After completing one time around, David decided to prepare for the long 100-yard swim toward the dock. He turned to Hassim and reassured him his balance would be paid upon his return to the Keys.

Hassim frowned.

"Okay. That's good provided you are successful and able to return!" Would you like my opinion Doctor Janus?"

David removed his shoes and said.

"Sure."

Hassim continued.

"Personally, I think your attempt to save your wife by yourself is insane! You don't know what you are up against...yes? ...There could be an army up there and I give you a zero to 20% chance of even reaching the complex on top of that hill, let alone getting inside. No doubt, these bad men are probably trained mercenaries. What chance do you think you have?"

David smiled sheepishly.

"Well Hassim…Probably no chance at all, but my wife is in there with those bastards. I have no choice but to try. It's win and take all, or die trying!"

Hassim dropped his head.

"Doctor you are a brave man and I offer my well wishes with your endeavors and good luck to you."

David climbed upon the transom and dove into the water. Hassim pulled away with the remaining engines still at idle, affording David the most amount of cover. The swim to the island was difficult. The winds picked up making the ocean topped with 3-foot whitecaps, forcing his efforts to make headway even more exhausting. David felt his strength weakening. He needed to stop more often than he wanted in order to regain his breath. He feared his muscles might cramp in the icy cold waters.

When he came close to the dock, he kept his head near the surface. The whitecaps and waves made sufficient noise at the shoreline to hide his approach.

Now he was 20-feet from his goal. He took a deep breath and tried to relax. He moved silently through the water and emerged next the moored speedboat. He moved slowly around the rim of the boat to make a quick analysis of anyone guarding the dock.

As David moved near a dock pilon, he observed one of the seal team guarding, holding an automatic weapon held close to his chest, military style.

Realizing he was already outgunned being without any weapon and barefoot besides, he returned to the speedboat hoping to find some sort of ordinance inside. He quietly slipped into the boat trying not to arouse the seal's attention. He crawled around inside to find a case strapped to the transom. He opened the clasp on the case and to his delight, there were more automatic weapons, two handguns and a bundle of hand grenades. He lifted one AR-15 assault rifle, 4 clips and one of the hand guns also with two clips. Took the grenade bundle and slung the bundle over his shoulder and quietly slipped back into the water. Now he felt much more confident he had leveled the playing field.

David's confidence waned when he spied the guard within close proximity. The idea he could successfully overtake this trained soldier seemed daunting. He knew a direct confrontation was out of the question. His only chance, an element of surprise. His mind raced to conceive a plan to somehow distract him long enough to approach from behind.

The beach did not present a sandy surface, but a graduation of small to large rocks distributed unevenly along the shore. The momentary idea was to toss a medium sized rock into the water, near the speedboat and lure him hopefully into a vulnerable location.

He took a breath to bolster his courage. He tossed the rock just behind the transom. The guard quickly spun around and scanned the area. He walked slowly toward the speedboat and to

David's delight, the soldier stepped into the boat approaching the transom to peer over the side. This was David's only chance. As the soldier leaned over to view the water, David took the assault rifle and swung it behind him causing him to buckle at the knees. Then while he had the soldier temporarily at a disadvantage he took the butt end of the rifle and bashed it against the soldier's head. Blood spurted from the back of his neck as he fell unconscious into the water. To ensure his success, he unstrapped the belt from the stock and wrapped it around the soldiers hands tying them behind his back, hoping he would drown before he awakened.

He thought. *'One down…how many more would there be?'*

Meanwhile inside the shadow Lab

Straker attached the magnetic interface over Sidoo's head. The magnetically based technology didn't require a close-fitting apparatus. Katie completed the reconstruction of her algorithms to be compatible with Straker's equipment. He attached the interface to the computer and switched on the system. Katie had to reorient the translation cyphers so Straker would leave Sidoo unharmed. Straker queried Sidoo immediately about the torqx technology. Sidoo resisted for several torturous sessions until he was so drained, he relented to give Straker the secrets he wanted.

Straker detached the electroencephalograph equipment he obtained from the MK-Ultra program, but left the bright Eye equipment attached to Sidoo's tank.

Straker declared.

"Well…as I promised… you will suffer an agonizing demise."

Straker continued.

"You see…I don't like any loose ends, or a trail for others to follow. You and the whale are collateral damage…Something about which I am accustomed."

Katie was tied up again with her feet together and hands behind her. Straker added.

"I would have Tom gag you, but there is no need for that anymore. Tom and Nick, …leave everything behind except the tape reels of course. Finish packing our gear and store all of it in the helicopter and fire it up. Lukas… you can drain the tank now. Jason, you and Craig will destroy the speedboat. We won't need it anymore. Tom… after Lukas finishes, place Dr. Janus in the tank and refill it."

Katie shouted at him.

"You bastard…You are the most despicable excuse for a human being I regret ever having met!"

Straker smiled at her and said finally.

"Charming as ever!"

At that moment, two explosions ripped through the side door. Half of the south wall of the complex collapsed into rubble. The explosion immediately killed Jason and Craig, leaving only Nick, Tom and Straker.

Straker said quickly.

"Okay boys…Looks like the Calvary has arrived…time to leave.

Sidoo struggled for a short time out of the water, with his last ounce of strength died.

Katie was lowered into the tank, now filling up. David acted quickly and fired upon Nick. The bullets striking him in the neck and chest caused him to drop to the ground. Meanwhile, Straker and Lukas mounted the helicopter with the blades reaching lift off speed.

David opened fire using the last three rounds of his assault weapon against the chopper but, the chopper continued to rise above the complex unaffected. Then he threw the assault weapon to the ground disgusted at his failure and watched helplessly, as the chopper turned toward the western slope of the complex.

David still felt determined to stop them, but how? Then he thought of the bundle of grenades still wrapped over his shoulder. He began to run like hell to reach the slope cliff before the helicopter reached the open sea. Moments before he reached the cliff summit, he removed the pins from the remaining grenades. This was the defining moment. His time now counted only in seconds. He would never again have another chance to stop the 'son of a bitch.'

As he reached the crest of the cliff, the chopper flew above and just past him. David slung the bandolero of grenades in one final thrust, and feeling like the fabled David against Goliath, the bandolero landed on the tail end of the landing runner. Moments later, the helicopter exploded killing all and destroying the cargo.

David sat down on the cliff and watched with some satisfaction, to see the remaining debris fall into the ocean. Suddenly, his mind flashed on Katie. He jumped up and ran toward the complex. Upon entering, he yelled out.

"Katie… where are you? …Katie, can you hear me …where are you, sweetie?"

Katie was completely submerged holding onto what little air remained in her lungs…she had given up being rescued. She resolved herself to her fate, her demise. David looked into the tank horrified. He dove in and swam to her and carried her to the surface.

He began to resuscitate her without even first removing her bonds. Several minutes went by but there was no response. He pumped against her heart and blew his vital air into her mouth many times. Tears began to stream down his cheeks while he felt devastated. He had to reconcile the fact he had lost her after all. He sat next to her lifeless body, cutting loose her bindings crying while she lay in his arms.

Then suddenly, she shook violently with deep coughing spasms.

"Oh baby…you're alive…thank the gods!"

Katie looked up at him wondering whether she was alive or just dead dreaming she was alive. She wrapped her arms around him crying.

"I had given up. I thought that you were not coming."

David reassured her.

"Yes baby…I almost didn't make it. We're going to be all right hon."

Bethesda Naval Hospital
Next day

Katie awoke in her hospital bed to see David looking fondly at her.

"Good morning sweetie. How you feeling after that horrible ordeal."

Katie looked at David and smiled.

"I'm feeling better. Well after all this, I will have to finally admit, you are my knight in shining armor, after all!"

David smiled at her with a bash Ville grin.

"I was highly motivated!"

"Honey…he continued… I want to stay with you for the rest of the day, but I have been summoned to the pentagon for a debriefing today, they want a full report."

Katie smiled squeezing his hand.

"knock'em dead tiger!"

Pentagon Office of Joint Chiefs

Admiral Jainway presided over the hearing.

"Well son…we congratulate you on your exploits to uncover Commander Straker's treachery. We are also greatly concerned about what you've learned regarding the whale dilemma.

"Unfortunately, Admiral…the data my wife and I collected was lost with the crash of the helicopter. But I am happy to report the whale related to us that the U.S.S. Scorpion incident was a simple case of self-defense. They bore no ill feelings towards our presence but expressed regret for our loss and ask that we do not use this technology anymore. It seems the Bright Eye technology has one terrible side effect…the signal it creates is lethal to all mammals in the ocean. Since they are an essential part of the ecosphere on the planet, I recommend it should not be used at all.

Admiral Jainway concluded.

"All right son…We'll consider their suggestions. Thank you for your service."

EPILOGUE

Bethesda Aquatic Lab

Reconstruction workers completed renovations of the lab in Bethesda, Maryland. Dr. David Janus returned to teaching as a tenured fellow at the Harvard School of Advanced Biological Sciences in Massachusetts. Though he planned to teach there three times a week, he would return to the lab in Bethesda to do his continued his fieldwork.

Dr. Kate Janus headed up the Department of Noetic and Neuro-linguistic Sciences also as a tenured fellow at Harvard. She would continue her experimental interspecies adaptive work both at the university while assisting Dr. Janus with his field work.

Twelve months passed since the U.S.S. Scorpion incident yet, there was still no sign of any whale species anywhere. Occasionally, bottlenose dolphins would appear in the bay near the lab.

The 89th Congress convened to ratify a proposal to the UN Council for the complete abolition of whale hunting internationally. Between the actions of an organization called Greenpeace and new UN sanctions against Japan forced the Japanese government to halt all whaling operations, leaving the open seas free and clear of any threat to the cetacean species.

Katie went to David's office to chat and suggested lunch to follow. She said.

"David…we haven't heard anything from the whales in many months. I have been wondering why that is…Perhaps they are still unsure of our intensions."

David replied.

"Yes …I am wondering that myself."

Katie continued to speak her thoughts out loud.

"Do you think there may be a reason behind it? Are they hurt or afraid to come out, or did they all leave before we could transmit our good news to them?"

David responded.

"Well… that is a good point. Perhaps they have retreated to an unknown place where they cannot be reached… They have essentially ignored our transmissions."

Katie went on.

"Bottlenose dolphins are also mammals.

Perhaps they know where the whales have gone?

…Maybe we should use them to relay our good will message."

David looked at her.

"That's a damn good idea, but our translator program is specific to the cetacean language… right?"

Katie paused to ponder…"Hmm…Let me see what can be done to adapt our program to the Gervais Delphinidin language."

David added."Let me know what you come up with…please."

Katie responded with a smile.

"You'll be the first to know my love."

Katie examined the language codex needed to communicate with the dolphins. As it turned out, after a few minor adjustments, she reported success with some of the dolphins on campus. Now the idea was to go to the lab in Maryland and try out her new algorithms.

David and Katie arrived early one night at the Bethesda Lab. She powered up the computers and loaded the new translation codex into the computers. David dropped the hydrophones into the saltwater viaduct at the lab which led to the open bay. They began to transmit hoping any dolphins in the neighborhood would respond.

'Hello…the man-child David and the woman-child Kate would like to call upon the pods of dolphins here, to exchange information.'

The 'hat' as they called it, was a neural network that stretched elastically and mounted Josephson conductors capable of converting their brainwaves into telepathic constructs. These probes linked to the computer interface and converted their thoughts into dolphin thought patterns.

They kept transmitting for several hours through the water but got no response.

Katie began to wonder if she missed something, or the dialect for the dolphins in the university was somehow different from the pod species in the bay.

It was later in the night after 1 am., that the first response came in.

'Hello …we are connecting to the man-child David and the woman child Kate…are you receiving us?'

David return first.

'*Hello…who is it that communes with us now?* '
The dolphin returned.

"We are of the Calle feyh clan…we are here to happily exchange information with the man-child clan.'

Katie began next.

"This is the woman-child Katie, we are very interested to reach the tomes of the whale clans… can you tell us where they have gone? …we want to exchange our tomes with them as well.'

'*The Calle Feyh are a collective consciousness…speaking to one of us is speaking to all. What do you want with the whale clans?* '

'*Please inform the whale clans it is safe to return to the great waters. The misinformation between our clans has been corrected…there will be peace between us…There will be no more devices used to create harm now.' The man-children regret the mistakes made by our clans that brought unspeakable harm to your kind'…Please inform the great Elder, Gandaloo Fah as well as the council Fah Ne we man-children vow an eternal peace within the greater Eternal Minoch of all water clans.* '

'Calle Feyh understands…we will convey your well wishes to our brothers.'

David and Katie heard nothing more from the dolphins that night. Their wish and hope for a renewed chance to begin, heralding a new world, a new earth where all species can live and thrive together in harmony and trust.

www.ingramcontent.com/pod-product-compliance
Lightning Source LLC
Chambersburg PA
CBHW071424200726
48294CB00002B/504